AMERICAN SPIRITS

AMERICAN SPIRITS

RUSSELL BANKS

 ALFRED A. KNOPF, NEW YORK, 2023

THIS IS A BORZOI BOOK
PUBLISHED BY ALFRED A. KNOPF

www.aaknopf.com

Knopf, Borzoi Books, and the colophon
are registered trademarks of Penguin Random House LLC.

Grateful acknowledgment is made to the following for permission
to reprint previously published material: An excerpt from "Closing Time"
by Leonard Cohen. Copyright © 1992 by Leonard Cohen.
Reprinted by permission of The Wylie Agency.

"Nowhere Man" was originally published in *Salmagundi*.
"Kidnapped" was originally published in *Conjunctions*.

Library of Congress Cataloging-in-Publication Data
Names: Banks, Russell, 1940–2023 author.
Title: American spirits / Russell Banks.
Description: First edition. | New York : Alfred A. Knopf, [2024] |
Identifiers: LCCN 2022054082 | ISBN 9780593536773 (hardcover) |
ISBN 9780593536780 (ebook)
Classification: LCC PS3552.A49 A74 2024 | DDC 813/.54—dc23
LC record available at https://lccn.loc.gov/2022054082

Jacket images (top to bottom): James Lange;
Chuck Pefley; Sonja Blom; all Alamy
Jacket design by Chip Kidd

Manufactured in the United States of America
First Edition

for Chase Twichell

CONTENTS

★

AMERICAN SPIRITS

NOWHERE MAN

THE WAY I HEARD, it started one Saturday morning when Doug was trying to sleep in, so as to sleep off another Friday night's overindulgence of alcohol down at the Spread Eagle, while Debbie kept the kids quiet in the basement. Debbie and the kids were decorating thank-you-for-your-service boxes to mail to the Fort Pierce reservists stationed over in Afghanistan. This was three years ago in the fall, before hunting season opened, or Doug would have been out early, which puts it near the end of October and shortly after the 10th Mountain 2nd Brigade got sent over to replace the 1st Brigade in order to participate in the U.S. counterterrorism mission against al-Qaida. Debbie and her St. Agnes's Ladies' Aid Society had learned how the winters in the mountains of Afghanistan were brutal and had spent the summer knitting wool hats and mittens and scarves for the 2nd Brigade reservists.

It wasn't crack of dawn early—nine-thirty or maybe ten—but Doug was still half-asleep, when the shooting from Zingerman's firing range broke into his slurry, hungover dreams like somebody popping popcorn in a microwave next to the bed. He flipped back the covers and for a moment sat slump-shouldered on the edge of the bed and felt his long, gaunt body fill with the sound of gunfire coming from the hills beyond the woods. Semiautomatic rifles, AR-15s and AK-47s, three or four at a time.

He stared out the bedroom window past his Ram pickup and Debbie's Forester at the pinched dry yellow lawn and the line of bony leafless birch trees that marked where his and Debbie's eight-acre lot ended and Zingerman's land—Doug's father's land—began. He stood and walked bare-assed and tousled down the hall to the bathroom, the whole way goddamning Yuri Zingerman and his fat-bellied, camoed, wannabe soldier boys. He peed and washed his face and berated the socialist Democrats and Governor Andrew Cuomo, along with the state police and the Essex County sheriff and the liberal members of the town select board and the tourist board, everyone in public office except the president, for refusing to shut down Zingerman's so-called firing range and military training center.

Debbie heard him overhead stomping around the bathroom barefoot and a few minutes later clumping in his boots in the kitchen, mumbling and grumbling to himself about the injustice of it, the hypocrisy, that's the word, the fucking *hypocrisy*. Down in the basement she couldn't herself hear the guns that had set Doug off and still fired in rackety waves like a series of full-on frontal assaults, but she was used to her husband's Saturday morning moods. She broke open a fresh pack of Crayolas and told Lannie and Leanne and Max to keep on writing their messages on the cards to our men and women in uniform while she checked on Daddy, and she'd come right back, and they'd fill the boxes together and later take them over to St. Agnes's for mailing and go by the schoolyard afterwards to play on the swings.

Max, the oldest, said he wanted to stay home, swings were for babies. Lannie and Leanne, the tow-headed boy and girl twins, punched his skinny arms from both sides and said they weren't babies, which they weren't, they were eight years old. Max said Dad promised to show him how to shoot this year when he goes deer hunting with Dad and Uncle Roy and Uncle Dave. Max can be on the drive, but by law he can't carry or shoot his own gun until he turns fifteen, still a few years off. Meanwhile he's legally old enough to shoot small game like squirrels and nuisance birds like starlings, as soon as Dad trains him on his Ruger 10/22, which fires ten rounds in less than thirty seconds, a gun with a scope, a gun that Dad promised to give to Max as soon as the boy proves he can handle its weight and recoil correctly.

Lannie and Leanne rolled their eyes and looked up at their mother as if pleading with her to shut their brother up. He'd been using their father's promise of the gun to lord it over the twins for weeks. It was as if he was repeatedly saying goodbye to them before going off to live with a different family, where he would have his own room in a newer, bigger house, where three kids didn't have to share one bedroom, where no one argued about money or wasting it at the Spread Eagle instead of saving it for groceries and school clothes and doctors' bills or building a garage. Lannie and Leanne wanted Max to hurry up and go live with that other family, so they could stop thinking about its existence and could make do with the mother and father they had.

Doug stood in his shirtsleeves on the deck off the kitchen, shivering from the cold and smoking a cigarette, staring in the direction of Zingerman's property. His long, mahogany-colored hair swirled in the wind. His hair and boney face and lanky build gave him the look of a rock musician, but he liked bluegrass and folk and played banjo in a four-man band with friends from high school and traveled several times a year to Virginia and the Carolinas to play in festivals.

Debbie slid open the glass door and said, "Aren't you freezing? Put on your jacket, Doug."

"There was a time," he said, "B-Z, before Zingerman, that is, there was a time when we had peace and quiet in abundance around here. When private property meant privacy. When a Dead End sign meant you didn't see downstate and out-of-state jerks driving SUVs and pickups past the house day and night and ORVs and ATVs trashing the woods and trails and scaring off the game. *Those were the days, my friend. We thought they'd never end,*" he sang to her. *"We'd sing and dance forever and a day."*

She stepped outside and plucked the cigarette from his hand and took a deep drag from it and passed it back to him. They both smoked, but agreed that smoking wasn't allowed inside the house or in front of the kids. They

smoked the same brand, "classic mellow" American Spirits in the yellow package. Smoking was something he and
Debbie shared. It gave them time alone together, which
they both still valued.

She wrapped her arms around herself against the cold
and watched him from behind as if taking his measure for
a coat. She was almost his height and had kept her figure despite three kids and was still regarded in town as a
beauty. Back when they first got together people spoke of
them as the perfect couple.

He said, "You could hear the wind in the pines and
birdsong, Debbie, instead of automatic gunfire. Which
Zingerman claims are just fireworks. Which we know
are homemade explosives he's using for blowing up old
wrecked cars that he's testing out in case he has to save the
world from socialism. There was a time, Deb, when deer
walked up to the deck and you could shoot the damned
creatures from the house in your stocking feet. Now, when
I want to kill a deer I got to put my boots on and drive over
to Walsingham or Starkville and hunt on somebody else's
land."

"Are you still drunk?"

He turned around and said, "What d'you mean, 'still'?"

Debbie took the cigarette out of Doug's hand and rubbed
it out in the cat food can they used for an ashtray.

He said, "I wasn't quite done with that, y'know."

She stepped back inside and slid the door shut and
started making Doug's late morning Saturday breakfast,
scrambled eggs and the pork chop he'd missed when he
didn't come home for supper. He followed her inside and

poured himself a cup of stale coffee and sat down at the table and waited for his breakfast. "Sorry," he said.

"For what?"

"I dunno. For being so touchy, I guess. Defensive."

"Touchy," she said. "Pissed is more like it, Doug. Call it what you want, 'touchy' or 'sensitive' or 'defensive.' But it's really pissed, isn't it?"

"Yeah, you're right. I am pissed," he said, as if he were naming his religion or his race. "It's why I like Trump. Which you don't seem to get. Trump, he's pissed, too. All those other guys, Obama and the Clintons and the Bushies, they just want us to get along in order to go along. Trump, though, he's freakin' pissed."

She put his plate in front of him and walked toward the basement door. "It's not about them, Obama and the Clintons and them. And it's not about Trump. He's not pissed, Doug. He's just acting like he's pissed. It's about you."

"Please," he said. "Don't start." She said something before returning to the basement, but Doug couldn't hear it above the steady, relentless hammering of the automatic weapons, even with the double-pane sliding glass door shut.

Zingerman's shooting range was a half mile farther up the narrow gravel lane that passed in front of his and Debbie's ranch house. When he and Debbie got married, Doug's father, Guy Lafleur, sold him the eight-acre lot for one dollar as a wedding present, and on weekends over the next three years Doug and his brothers-in-law, Roy and Dave, built their house where the lane ended and their land began. After Doug's dad died, Doug and his two sisters, Nina and Tracy, and their husbands, Roy and Dave, his brothers-in-law and hunting companions, sold off the rest of the old man's land, all 320 acres. It was the last large tract of undeveloped forested land inside the town limits. They sold it to Yuri Zingerman from New Jersey. He said he wanted it for a private hunting preserve, but promised Doug that he and Roy and Dave could continue to hunt on the property. Zingerman said he was a veteran of the IDF, the Israel Defense Forces, but he talked with a regular American accent. He ran a company in New Jersey that provided security for celebrities and professional athletes and business executives. It was impressive when he named who they were.

Doug, who worked as a full-time caretaker for summer residents and a part-time handyman in the winter months, spent his share of the cash sale of his dad's land on a new Dodge Ram pickup and paid off the mortgage on the house. Without the mortgage hanging over them, he figured he could support the family with his caretaking and seasonal work as a handyman, and maybe in a year or two he could build a third bedroom onto the house and the two-car garage Debbie wanted. They could get off food stamps and buy health insurance. When the twins were old enough for Debbie to go back to waitressing full time instead of part time, which should be soon, they'd be sitting pretty. That's how he put it to anyone who'd listen, with his lips pursed in an air kiss. Sitting pretty.

For a few years Zingerman showed up only during deer hunting season and sometimes came for a week or two earlier to shoot birds, usually alone or in the company of a couple of New Jersey hunting buddies, and stayed in town at the Bide-a-Wile. Then one fall he cut some trees in the center of his forested acreage and built a rough one-room hunting camp that was accessible by ATV from in front of Doug's place, where Zingerman parked his black GMC Yukon Denali. The next year he cut more trees and put down a gravel extension of Lafleur Lane and installed a corrugated metal bridge over Blackstone Kill and a thirty-two-foot-long RV. The following year he added a single-wide mobile home.

The Dead End sign at the turnoff from Route 50 was still there, but now Lafleur Lane continued past where it used to end at Doug and Debbie Lafleur's house and dipped down to the banks of Blackstone Kill and crossed the creek on Zingerman's bridge, switchbacked uphill through pines and spruce and ended deep in the woods at a circular turnaround in front of Zingerman's single-wide and the RV parked next to it and a barn-sized garage where he kept his vehicles and the fenced-in yard where he kept his dogs.

In winter the road agent for the town of Sam Dent, Doug's brother-in-law Dave Fitzgerald, plowed the lane, courtesy of the taxpayers, state and local, but only as far as Debbie and Doug's driveway. Zingerman by then had become a year-round resident of Sam Dent, albeit one who spent a lot of time away, presumably running his New Jersey business, Zip-Tie Security. He maintained the rest of the lane himself with his own trucks and plows and posted

it with Private Property, No Hunting, and No Trespassing
signs. Power and phone lines only went as far as Debbie
and Doug's place. Yuri Zingerman was living off the grid.

You'll want to know what he was like, Yuri Zingerman. I
ran into him a couple of times in town early on. The car
he rode in on only reinforced our first impression—New
Jersey plates, a block-long, black Denali with tinted windows, possibly armor plated. He was a short, blocky man,
wearing one of those Jewish caps, a yarmulke, which you
don't see here very often. Otherwise he was dressed like
a regular local guy in camo and jeans and insulated vest,
although you knew right away he wasn't local, because of
the yarmulke and the way he held his body, like it was a
chisel waiting for a hit from a hammer. He had no discernible body fat, but did not seem particularly muscular. Just
hard, as if carved from a chunk of stone. He was in his
early or midthirties, and his face was bronzed, like he'd visited a tanning salon, which stood out, because it was early
spring then and nobody was tanned. We figured he must've
spent time in someplace like Miami or Las Vegas. He had
a buzzed haircut and a thick black mustache and matching
eyebrows that were almost connected in the middle and
squinty blue eyes with crinkles in the corners and a cleft
chin. He wore a small diamond stud in the lobe of his left
ear. If he didn't seem so hostile and foreign, you could say
that he was conventionally handsome, because his face was
symmetrical and clean cut.

The morning he first showed up in town, the Noonmark Diner was crowded, all the tables taken, as usual. Zingerman checked out exactly where everyone was seated and simultaneously rejected them, as if the tables were empty and he was deliberately choosing not to sit at any of them. He chose instead to sit on a stool at the counter, squeezing in alongside a half dozen local workmen who were getting ready to head out to their job sites, and he spread a give-away real estate sales pamphlet out in front of him and read it like it was a newspaper.

When Debbie came up to take his order, he spoke to her in a surprisingly soft voice. This was right after she'd married Doug and before the kids. They had closed on buying the eight acres from Doug's dad, and Doug had already dug the cellar and put in the cinderblock foundation for the house, and she was waitressing full time at the Noonmark. Debbie was just twenty then, and with that red hair and gray eyes and perfect teeth and her height, she could've been a model. She had a wicked sense of humor and didn't take herself too seriously, so most of the male customers liked to flirt with her, especially the first time they met her and she hadn't had a chance to verbally flip them off yet.

No playing around for Zingerman, though. He ordered two poached eggs and asked about the raisin English muffins. "Are they homemade?" he said. "I read the Noonmark Cafe is famous for their homemade muffins and pies."

She lied and said, "Yes. Homemade."

He gave her a thin smile like he knew she was lying. He said, "Well, okay, I'll have a corn muffin instead. Toasted."

"It's Noonmark Diner," she said, "not Cafe," and went back to the kitchen.

When she brought him his eggs and corn muffin and re-filled his coffee cup, he pointed to the real estate pamphlet. "Who among these do you think is the most honest realtor in town?"

In a flat voice she said, "They're all honest," trying not to sound insulted, although she knew that none of them was wholly honest, just a person in business, a person try-ing to make a living, like everybody else.

Sam Dent is not the kind of town where a few people make a killing and the rest are on welfare. Here everyone gets by, just barely—except for the summer residents and Yuri Zingerman, people who make their money elsewhere in ways that are mysterious to people like Debbie and Doug and the other locals.

On his own, Zingerman found a realtor he trusted not to screw him, which wasn't hard. Most of them, as Debbie said, were honest. And although he was obviously a man with plenty of disposable income and from away, a flat-lander, as the locals say, he was not a man a realtor wanted to lie to. With the blunt force of his personality and his sharp-edged physical presence, he made people deal hon-estly with him. We heard he wrote a personal check to Doug and his sisters for a quarter-million dollars for the 320 acres they'd inherited from their father, and for a while there were no problems between him and the town and between him and Doug and Debbie. As soon as his check cleared, Zingerman posted the acreage with the No Hunt-ing, No Trapping, No Trespassing signs, but he told Doug that he could continue to hunt the land, sometimes with Roy and Dave, the same as he had since he was Max's age.

In return, at Zingerman's request, Doug patrolled the

property during and out of season, as if it still belonged to his father or all of it still belonged to him and his sisters, warning off it anyone from town or elsewhere who wanted to hunt there, as he had always done. Except that now he carried a typed letter from Yuri Zingerman that said Douglas Lafleur was authorized by the owner, Yuri Zingerman, to expel anyone who did not have written permission to hunt on this property. If said person refused to leave the property, Douglas Lafleur was instructed to have said person arrested for trespassing.

Then there was that strange confrontation at the Spread Eagle. It was right after Columbus Day, an unseasonably warm night, one of the special once-a-month occasions which Doug and Debbie called Date Night that they set aside for hiring a babysitter and going out together without Max and the twins. "Date Night, it's designed to save the marriage," Debbie told her three closest female confidantes at the St. Agnes Ladies' Aid Society. "You ought to try it." Side by side at the buffet table in the church annex recreation room, sorting and bagging groceries donated to the Sam Dent food pantry for families in need, the women had smiled and nodded in sympathetic approval. Half the town takes care of the other half or at least donates a month's time or income to the care and feeding of those who have nothing to donate. It's a form of tithing.

Standing at the bar, Doug ordered his third gin and tonic and another beer for Debbie and said, "I get to hunt there,

Debbie, which is like I'm hunting my own land. My dad's and my granddad's land. And Roy and Dave, them, too, as long as they're with me."

Debbie said, "What kind of deal is that? You're not his caretaker. You're like his private forest ranger. Only he's not paying you, Doug."

"The right to hunt is not nothing for something, y'know."

This was back before strangers every weekend started driving past the house on their way to Zingerman's, most of them in SUVs and pickups with out-of-state plates, some flying Confederate flags, their bumpers and tailgates plastered with stickers promoting gun rights and libertarian slogans like Don't Tread on Me and Live Free or Die and Christian references to apocalyptic biblical verses. This was before the automatic weapons and the explosions, when it was still possible to hunt the property and kill a deer. It was before Doug, and especially Debbie, decided that Zingerman might be dangerous.

The truth is, on those date nights Debbie wasn't trying to save their marriage. She was trying to save her husband from his drinking. Back then no one except Debbie thought Doug had a problem with alcohol. He was just a happy, weekend drunk, a smiling noncombatant who, after his third or fourth gin and tonic, enjoyed playing around with words, twisting and stretching their meanings like they were made of taffy. When he was sober, which even she had to admit was most of the time, he was reticent and slow to speak, one of those men whose body seems more intelligent than his mouth. A few drinks into an evening at the Spread Eagle, however, and Doug Lafleur would come off as the smartest, funniest guy in the place. Caitlin Mungo, the owner, kept her late husband Sam's banjo behind the bar solely for Doug, who toward the end of the evening was happy to play and sing Leonard Cohen's "Closing Time" for the few remaining celebrants, and afterwards everyone would head out to their cars and trucks, humming the song.

> The fiddler fiddles something so sublime
> All the women tear their blouses off,
> And the men they dance on the polka-dots,
> And it's partner found, it's partner lost
> And it's hell to pay when the fiddler stops:
> It's closing time . . . clos-ing time.

Debbie took a seat by the screened door to catch the autumn evening breeze and watched Doug get warmed up with the kid bartender and a half dozen customers at the bar, telling them his story of driving from Sam Dent over Iron Mountain to Port Henry on a snowy late February night back in 2012 in a van with Larry Gaines and three of his and Larry's friends and Doug's brothers-in-law, Roy and Dave Fitzgerald. They were on a sacred mission, he told them. They were off to collect Larry's winnings in the Super Bowl pool at the Lake Monster Tavern, a basement dive somewhat notorious for the owner's collection of Nazi regalia—helmets and Luftwaffe flight caps and flags and banners and swastika armbands—that hung on the walls and around the mirror behind the bar.

Ten days after the game, Super Bowl XLVI, Larry had found, tucked into his overstuffed wallet, the fifty-dollar ticket with the winning score, Giants over the Patriots, 21–17, that he thought he'd lost. When he went alone to the Lake Monster to collect his winnings, the owner, Regis Warriner, who'd organized the pool and held the $1,250 pot, told him that it was too late for Larry to make his claim, and there was no proof that he'd kicked his fifty bucks into the pool, anyhow. Warriner told Larry that since there was no declared legal winner, he had rolled the whole amount into next year's pool. If Larry wanted a piece of that, it was going to cost him another fifty bucks to play.

"So we stroll into the Lake Monster," Doug continued, "all seven of us, with little Larry Gaines invisible in the rear. You know how he disappears when he's with normal-sized people. Anyhow and otherwise, it's like the Lake Monster is the fucking OK Corral and we're the Earp brothers and Doc Holliday and Johnny Ringo come looking for the Clanton Boys. None of us'd stepped foot into that Nazi cave before, except for Larry, who'd been working construction in Port Henry that winter, and the Lake Monster regulars are all giving us these hard-assed SS looks. We part them like the Red Sea, and little Larry steps between us and bellies up to the bar, like he's a Big Dog now, and Regis Warriner looks us over, and he greets him like they're soul mates, twin brothers separated at birth and at last reunited, and, jeez, ever since the Super Bowl, Regis says, he's been waiting for the chance to give Larry his winnings, but just didn't know how to reach him."

Knowing laughter from Doug's listeners—when the screened door next to Debbie swung open, and Yuri Zingerman entered. Rarely sighted at the Spread Eagle, he was thought to do his drinking alone or maybe with his New Jersey and downstate cronies at his hunting camp in Lafleur's Woods. Doug stopped telling his story, and the place dropped into silence.

Debbie said, "Doug, let's go now. The babysitter . . ."

Doug turned and gave Zingerman a wide, welcoming smile. "Wow! It's the high plains drifter, and he's come to town! Let me buy you a drink, Drifter," he said and waved him over to the bar.

Zingerman walked across the room and came in close to Doug. He lifted his upper lip, more a grimace than a half smile. In a thin voice he said, "No, thanks. I stopped by your place to speak with you about something. The kid, the babysitter, she told me you'd be here."

"Sure you won't let me buy you a drink?"

"I don't drink."

Doug got suddenly somber, as if from slightly hurt feelings. "O-kay," he said. "What's on your mind, then?"

The two men stood facing each other, Doug leaning down and forward as if to hear better, the shorter, blockier Zingerman looking at Doug's throat, as if targeting it. Doug's audience had backed away to give the two some space to speak in private.

Debbie called over, "Doug, we promised the babysitter. We ought to go now."

Zingerman said, "You planning to hunt on my land this season?"

"Well, yeah."

"Forget about it. I don't want anyone hunting there anymore. Even you."

"What?"

"You heard me." Zingerman turned and started to move away. Doug reached out and with his thumb and forefinger held on to the loose sleeve of Zingerman's plaid flannel shirt, but before he could tug it, Zingerman pinned Doug's offending hand to the bar and had Doug bent backwards against the bar, off-balance, knees buckling, his free hand flailing the air, Zingerman's hand wrapped around Doug's throat, so that Doug was looking up at the ceiling, unable to breathe.

A second later, Zingerman released him. Doug stared up at Zingerman in a mix of relief and disbelief, his eyes filling with tears. He touched his throat gingerly, looking for a wound to explain the pain. He tried to speak, but couldn't make a sound.

It all happened too fast for anyone to say or do anything to stop or slow it. No one in the place moved or said a word as Zingerman walked past Debbie and out to his big Denali idling in front and got in and drove off.

Debbie rushed across the room to Doug and said, "My God, honey, are you okay?" and examined his throat, which was red from Zingerman's grip, but appeared to be uninjured. A few people, including Caitlin, the owner, and the young guy tending bar said things like "Jesus Christ!" and "What the hell was that all about?" and "What'd you do to piss him off like that, Doug?"

When he could speak again, Doug leaned away from Debbie and gave a little laugh and said, "He don't . . . Zingerman don't like anyone touching him . . . uninvited. I guess."

Debbie took him by the arm and led him out the door to her Forester. She got in on the driver's side, Doug, unprotesting, the passenger's. She said, "What did he say to you?"

"He don't . . . he don't want me hunting Pop's land anymore."

"He say why?" She started the engine and pulled out of the parking lot onto the road and headed toward home, five miles east of the village center. Doug didn't answer. It was shortly after nine, and the winding two-lane road was empty of vehicles. The white center stripe flashed into the spray of the headlights and disappeared into the darkness behind. Doug half opened the passenger-side window and inhaled. The wet smell of an approaching lake-effect snowstorm out of Ontario mingled with the odor of mouldering leaves blown off the trees by wind and rain the week before. Fall was slipping into winter. Deer hunting season.

He tried to replay in his mind what had happened—Zingerman pinning Doug's hand to the bar and rendering him helpless, knees buckled, his free hand grasping at air, and Zingerman's ability to do it so quickly that Doug couldn't see it happening until it was already over and done. It mystified Doug. It somehow gratified a desire he didn't know he had and left him strangely satisfied afterwards. He couldn't remember the actual event beyond reaching out and catching Zingerman's shirtsleeve between the thumb and forefinger of his left hand. All he remembered was Zingerman turning around, presenting a blurred image of his face, impassive, expressionless, almost bored looking, and Doug's own body suddenly off-balance, no longer under his control, steered backwards and down, his offending left hand, palm up, clamped to the bar, open and ready for a spike to be driven through it straight and deep into the wood, the right hand extended as if trying in vain to avoid sharing the fate of the left, trying to escape the arm and shoulder it was attached to. He did recall Zingerman's left hand locked on his throat, the thumb pressing the carotid artery, the fingers closing on his windpipe, a black halo closing in on Zingerman's cold face.

And just as suddenly, Zingerman was gone, and Doug saw that the spike had been pried out of the wooden bar, and his left hand had been sewn back onto the arm and the arm onto the shoulder, and he could draw air back into his lungs again, blood into his brain. The black halo faded to gray, and the lights came up as at the end of a movie, leaving him feeling strangely sated, as if something long desired had finally come to him in an unanticipated form with unimagined content. It was exactly what he had hoped for. Not so much the thing itself, Zingerman's sudden inexplicable dominance of him, but the thrilled feeling aroused in his chest afterwards, when he began to breathe again, the buoyancy in his captured and released left hand, the restful peace of his right hand settled at his side, the return of his body to his body after having been briefly absent.

Doug remained silent until they pulled into their driveway. Debbie shut off the engine and sighed. "This is the second winter we were going to have a two-car garage," she said.

"He can go straight to hell if he thinks I'm not hunting on Pop's land."

"Who? It's not Pop's anymore, remember?"

"No. It'll always be Pop's. Just like it'll always be Grand-pop's. That's why people call it Lafleur's Woods. Those two old boys, Pop and Grandpop, they'd roll over in their graves if they thought me and Roy and Dave couldn't hunt that land. Max, too. Max's gonna get his chance to hunt those woods, just like I did when I was his age. And my dad before me. And Grandpop. That sonofabitch Zingerman, he can have his hunting camp out there if he wants, he paid for that right, but he can't keep me from tramping across those ridges and creeks that I know like the lines of my own hand and killing a deer once a year and busting up a few coveys of partridges and quails. It's my goddamn birthright."

She was silent for a moment. She knew that he'd had three gin and tonics and had been publicly humiliated by Zingerman, but even if he were stone-cold sober and Zingerman had managed to be polite and had apologized for posting the land and barring him from hunting it, Doug would be threatening to kill his deer over there anyway. He was a man. That's what men do. She knew that by tomorrow he'd be trying to talk Zingerman out of his decision, and by Monday he'd be grumbling about Zing-erman's decision, and when hunting season opened, he'd meet up early with Dave and Roy, and they would hunt on somebody else's land, not Zingerman's. Not Pop's and Grandpop's.

She said, "Seriously, Doug, when are we going to get the garage built? We can't go another whole year without it."

★

It snowed twice that week, six inches, then another three—heavy wet snow that half melted during the days and refroze at night and got wetter and heavier as the week went on. At first Doug did as Debbie predicted. He called Zingerman and tried to talk him into letting him and his brothers-in-law continue to hunt his father's and grandfather's land. That was Monday.

Zingerman said forget it. "Nobody's going to be hunting there from now on. I got different uses for the land," he said. He wanted to know how Doug got his phone number.

Doug said he looked it up online. He didn't say, but Debbie had done the search for him. "It's posted on your company's website," he said. "Zip-Tie Security, Inc."

"It's a business number," Zingerman said. "I don't usually answer, but my secretary's out sick."

"From your website, that's quite the business you're running, Yuri. I mean, 'Penetration room clearing.' 'Deep conceal holster training.' 'Israeli security training package.' I don't know what half those terms mean, but it's pretty impressive."

"You wanna take one of my courses, Doug? You could use one, judging from the other night." He gave a short, cold laugh. "You oughtn't grab a man from behind unless you're prepared to take him down. Lesson number one, Doug. No charge."

Doug said no, he wasn't interested in any of those courses. He was only interested in killing one deer a year for himself and one each for his brothers-in-law, Roy and Dave Fitzgerald. He tried to explain how hunting culled the herd and was a good conservation practice or the deer would overpopulate and start to starve, but Zingerman cut him off.

"Look, we got nothing to talk about. I'm putting in a shooting range, it's part of my business, and I'll be bringing clients in for advanced training. Last thing I need is local deer hunters wandering around the place and accidentally stepping into the line of fire. They don't sell insurance for that, Doug. You're a good guy, be a good neighbor, okay?"

It was more a warning than a request. Zingerman clicked off before Doug could respond, which Doug realized later was lucky, because he was about to say that he planned on hunting his dad's and granddad's woods anyhow. And he was bringing Roy and Dave, and if anyone was going to accidentally step in the line of fire, it was likely to be him, Zingerman, or one of his so-called clients, not Doug and his brothers-in-law, and in fact, he was so confident of their safety and Zingerman's lack thereof, he was going to bring his eleven-year-old son, Max, to help drive the deer. He wanted his boy to learn the deers' bedding spots and trails the same way that he and Roy and Dave had acquired intimate knowledge of such things from a lifetime of hunting those same woods.

He thought that if he said it right, this information might soften Zingerman's heart. It took him another full day before he realized that it would not have been useful to let Zingerman know in advance that he and his son and his brothers-in-law would be hunting his dad's and granddad's land this coming weekend. No point in forewarning him. It was late Friday afternoon, almost dark at 5:30. He and Debbie were drinking beer and smoking together on the back deck off the kitchen, standing side by side, gazing in the direction of the dusky woods. Zingerman's woods. Lafleur's Woods.

"We'll just go in there early the first day of the season and take out our deer, and the hell with him," he told Debbie. "He'll never even know we done it."

"Doug, that's about as dumb a thing as you've ever thought of doing."

"Sometimes you got to do a foolish thing in order to do the right thing," he said.

"I'm not letting Max go with you."

"Whoa. When it comes to educating the boy to hunting, I'll say when he's ready. It's a lifelong process, and it starts now for him. He's ready to drive the deer, or at least watch how it's done. He won't carry a gun for four more years, but he's got a lot he can learn before then. I started carrying a gun a lot younger than that, y'know. Of course, that was before the government started chipping away at the Second Amendment," he added.

"Please, don't start," she said. "What if Zingerman . . . ?"

"What if Zingerman what? Worst he can do is call the state police, and by the time they arrive, we're back here at the house butchering a deer we can say we shot in the yard from the deck in our stocking feet."

"What's that going to teach Max? That it's okay to lie to the police?"

"The staties all know me and Roy and Dave. They don't care where we shot our deer. They don't like Zingerman any more than we do. Actually, the one I want to be teaching is Zingerman. He's the one needs a lesson. Coming into our town like this and snatching out of circulation three hundred twenty acres of prime hunting grounds. And I want Max to know we aren't gonna let him get away with it. I want the whole damn town to know it. And the state police, too."

"You're the one who sold him the land. You and your sisters."

"Yeah, but we had a deal. It's him who changed the rules. And I'm just saying no, that's all. No, dammit. No."

This was not like Doug. He was an accommodating man, a soft man—nonconfrontational, as they say. Debbie was not accustomed to him opposing her like this, firm and stubbornly irrational. Pigheaded. She was unsure how to get him to back off. It must have to do with that weird confrontation the other night between him and Zingerman at the Spread Eagle, she thought. Or was it something else? She didn't buy Doug's sudden sentimental attachment to his father's and grandfather's land. Where'd that come from? He'd been all too happy to join his sisters, Nina and Tracy, when they had the chance to sell the land to Zingerman, and they would have done it even if Zingerman hadn't promised not to subdivide or develop it and hadn't given them permission to hunt there. Doug wanted the money. He needed the money, not the land. They all did.

Maybe Zingerman's website set him off on this tangent. They probably shouldn't have studied it so carefully, but the website was strangely fascinating to them both. It told them a lot about Zingerman that they hadn't known before—its ridiculous, pumped-up masculinity and all those videoed self-defense fantasies of middle-aged White men with stubbled beards disabling scary strangers who looked like the young Osama bin Laden with jujitsu or karate or whatever Israeli martial art Zingerman was teaching, and the muscular men in tight sleeveless tees, like characters out of the video games that Max is always asking for but they refuse to buy for him, pulling a concealed pistol from a quick-draw holster and crouching and pretending to spray a windowless cinderblock room with bullets, instantly killing bodyguards and family members who happen to be off-camera and are presumed to be armed and dangerous, wearing explosive vests.

Doug was behaving like a child, she thought. Maybe Zingerman and his website made him feel like a child, maybe that's the point of the website, its sales pitch, and Doug doesn't like the feeling, he hates it, and wants to shake it off like a dog coming out of the water after a swim. She almost felt sorry for her husband.

"Just promise me you won't take Max into the woods with you," she said and rubbed out her cigarette.

Doug said, "It's no more dangerous for the boy without Zingerman's permission than it was going to be with it. You had no problem with the idea then. No, I made Max a promise, and I intend to keep it."

During the night a sudden thaw slipped in from the southeast. Before dawn the nine inches of heavy wet snow on the ground shed a low, silvered, cloud-like fog that hovered above the terrain, head-high in the pale light, blocking the hunters' view through the trees and brush. Doug and the boy kept their gaze directly in front of them, fixed on the fist-sized cloven hoofprints of the big male and on the smaller tracks of the females and yearlings and fawns. They didn't look to see where the tracks led and didn't intend to follow them until the fog lifted or burned off. Doug doubted the day would turn out to be warm and sunlit anyhow or cold and wintry, either. He thought the fog would last and shorten their sight line to fifty feet the whole day. It was not an uncommon phenomenon at this time of year, falling as it did halfway between autumn and winter and not fully either one.

In a voice barely above a whisper, he said, "We ain't gonna shoot at what we can't see. Your uncles are out there driving that bad boy and his ladies downwind back to their hidey-hole here."

Doug and Max had spooked the buck and the does—they had sighted and counted three, but from the tracks Doug was sure there were more. Possibly five or six. After the animals' rumps and flashing white tails had disappeared into the fog, Doug sat down on the thick, moss-covered trunk of a fallen oak tree twenty or so feet from where the deer had nestled overnight and laid his rifle across his lap and patted the place on the log next to him on his left, away from his shooting side, for the boy to sit down, too. He showed the boy the different tracks and differentiated their size and calculated the varied weights of the deer that had put them down.

"When he comes back, he won't know we're here till he's close enough to see our boots."

The boy said, "That's when you'll shoot him, right?"

Doug nodded and said, "No more talking."

The two sat in silence and waited for Roy and Dave to cross above Blackstone Kill on the sedimented rock bed a third of a mile upstream from Zingerman's iron bridge. Roy and Dave had arrived at six and parked their pickups in Doug's driveway in the dark, and when they all went out at dawn, the brothers had split off from him and Max at the gate where the lane left Doug's eight acres and entered Zingerman's 320. By now Roy and Dave would be trudging in heavy wet snow up the steep side of the ridge or slipping and sliding down the slope beyond, passing along the line of white pines toward the poplars that crowded the fogged-in swampy headwaters of the kill.

Doug and his brothers-in-law knew that the deer, roused from their hole, would head uphill for the poplar grove at the headwaters. They knew that the herd would hear Dave's and Roy's hard breathing from the climb to the ridge and their long descent to the bowl-shaped muskeg on the other side, and they would smell the men coming. The men knew that the herd would nervously bunch up and huddle in the poplar grove for a moment, and then, led by the buck, would circle back down to where Doug and his son sat waiting.

For seventy-some years this forest was the Lafleur family's private hunting preserve. Before that, for a hundred years it was a Boston-based timber company's wilderness cache of uncut trees, part of the land across the region that got auctioned off in the 1930s and '40s for pennies an acre when the company shifted operations south, and in 1947

Doug's grandfather had bought a chunk of it. Before that, before the American settlers and the British and the French Canadians and the Dutch, for ten thousand years it was the Mohawks' and Mi'kmaqs' home ground. Doug liked thinking about that. He liked calling up that long line of woodsmen and hunters. He liked to believe that he was descended from them, that his relation to this piece of the earth matched theirs, that he knew in all seasons its streams and brooks and swamps, its glacial forests changing from hardwoods to dark conifers to ferny sunlit patches, that he knew it fully as well as those old-time hunters did, and he knew the man-made trails and paths laid down over centuries on top of the trails and paths followed for millennia by the animals before the humans made their way here, and he knew the behavior and habits and needs and desires of all the animals and birds that lived in the forest.

Without that ancient connection to the land, who was Doug Lafleur, anyhow? No one. Nothing. Just a not very talented amateur musician hanging around this small town for a lifetime, finding easy ways to house and feed his wife and kids and spending too much time at the local tavern amusing his neighbors with tall tales and dumb songs, a man with no good reason to be living and working here instead of somewhere else. Christ, anywhere. And no matter where he lived and worked, wouldn't it be the same?

A nowhere man, that's what he'd become. Like the guy in the Beatles' song.

It was a mistake to sell the land to Zingerman, he said to himself. A mistake to sell it to anyone. He and his sisters should have clung to it for another generation for Max and his cousins to grow up on. It wasn't fair to blame the old man, but Doug's father had started the process by selling Doug the eight-acre pie-shaped corner adjacent to Route 50. The old man at first didn't want to sell off the flat, birch-covered stretch of ground, but Doug, newly married, wanted to build his own house, even if he had to borrow fifty thousand from the bank to do it. He talked the old man into signing over the eight acres for a dollar an acre so he could use the appraised value of the land, a thousand times what he'd paid for it, to guarantee the bank loan. Doug and his father thought they were outsmarting the bankers.

They never should have done it, though. No one outsmarts the bankers. With help from his brothers-in-law over the next three years he built the one-story, two-bedroom bungalow with a full basement, and though he knew he could have done it cheaper with a double-wide set on cinderblocks, he wouldn't have been able to expand on a double-wide, someday adding a third bedroom and a two-car garage with a tool room, the same as he could on a regular house. With his meager income from caretaking the homes of summer residents and handyman work over the winter, the mortgage payments turned out to be more than he could afford—several years into it and he was still paying mostly interest, and the principal was down barely seven hundred dollars from the fifty thousand he'd borrowed, and recently he'd been falling behind and was being charged penalties for late payments.

After the old man died he never should have agreed with Nina and Tracy to sell the rest of the land in order to pay off the bank loan with his third of the inheritance.

He could have somehow figured out a way to make the mortgage payments by taking a night shift at one of the resort hotels or a factory job in one of the larger towns downstate. Or he and Debbie could have sold the house instead and rented an apartment or a house in town. They might have saved enough that way to afford health insurance. And after they sold their father's land, he shouldn't have bought the new pickup. He could have squeezed a couple more years' use from his old rust bucket of a truck. He and his sisters would still own the Lafleur Woods, the headwaters of Blackstone Kill, the sedimented shale slabs cut crosswise by the kill and the ridges and gullies, the moraines and eskers and erratics and the rock-strewn till left behind by the retreating glaciers ten thousand years ago. He'd still be able to hunt on his ancestors' land. This love of the land, this irrational claim on it, was Doug's strength, and it was his weakness.

Doug and the boy sat side by side on the fallen oak tree at the edge of the herd's abandoned bedding of mashed grass and brush, the boy half asleep, eyes closed, Doug listening to the Beatles tune, unable to remember all the words, unable to stop the lines of the chorus from replaying in his ears over and over again, when the black rack of antlers and chestnut shoulders and chest and head of the buck emerged from the pale fog that surrounded them. Doug counted twelve points and guessed 180 pounds. He held off a few seconds and made no motion or sound to alert the boy, who might have jumped at the sight of the big deer so near to them, turning the animal, spoiling Doug's shot. He wanted to make it a head shot, a single bullet from his .30-06 that would drop the buck where he stood, deadly and clean and on open ground for ease of gutting him afterwards. The buck was upwind of the man and the boy, and the fog obscured the animal's vision even more than it did theirs, for they were motionless and seated low on the log close to the snow-covered ground and the buck was stepping forward at the front of his herd of females and yearlings and fawns, looking for danger from his standing height.

Doug studied the animal's large, dark, pond-deep eyes and waited another thirty seconds, as the buck scanned the area and saw no threat and came closer, and then, when he was barely a dozen feet away, Doug saw the buck's eyes widen and ears pivot toward them and he knew the buck had spotted them, and without a conscious thought, while still seated, Doug reacted as if instinctively, although it was a long-trained, coordinated sequence of actions performed by every part of his body, his shoulders and arms and hands, his abdomen and back, his eyes and ears and his heart and lungs, too. He was able in that instant to stop his breath and slow his heartbeat, macro and micro movements all coordinated in a single swift action that he had practiced a thousand times since boyhood and had relied on for killing deer and birds and varmints, raccoons and coyotes, and putting down injured animals and livestock raised for meat by his neighbors and old sick family pets, a thousand times of bringing the barrel of the gun up, sighting down its length, squeezing the trigger—

The buck went down, chest first. Then his whole huge body crumpled into the snow, his thick neck suddenly gone slack, his head lolled to one side, and his herd of adult females and their fawns and yearling does and bucks scattered back into the deep woods.

The gunshot startled Max from his slumber. He had not seen his father kill the deer, although he believed that he had witnessed it. His father said, "We have to move him." He leaned his rifle against the forked trunk of a young birch and grabbed the buck below the dewclaws of his hind legs and dragged the body of the animal across the clearing to a slope nearby and positioned the body of the animal with its hind end down, its head pointed uphill.

Doug explained to the boy that you need to move the deer and gut him quickly while the body is still warm and limber. "And you want to tilt him on a little hill like this, if you can find one. So when you open him up everything inside spills out and runs downhill."

As he worked, he explained to his son what he was doing and why. It was important for the boy to learn early that there was a lot more to hunting than firing your gun and killing something. "You have to give a lot of care to what you kill," he said.

He unsheathed his hunting knife with the gut hook and made a shallow surgical incision that cut through the deer's hide without cutting the stomach muscles. He sliced beneath the skin to where the animal's chin would begin if he had a chin and came back to his original incision and cut all the way down to the deer's anus. He cut carefully through the belly muscle and placed two fingers of each hand into the incision and pulled the muscle away from the stomach and intestines, and with the gut hook on his knife he opened the rest of the belly, cutting all the way down to the anus again. He sliced off the penis and laid it gently aside in the snow. He moved up the body to the rib cage and cut through the ribs along the sternum with the short blade of his bone saw.

He was sweating now, and he rubbed his forehead with the back of his bare, bloody hand and asked Max to pull his handkerchief from his back pants pocket and wipe his face for him. He spread the chest cavity open with both hands and showed the animal's diaphragm muscle to Max. "It's what separates the heart and the lungs from the digestive organs," he said. "You got to cut it, but you want to be careful and not puncture anything." He reached into the chest cavity and up and found the esophagus and cut it free of the throat and pulled out the remaining connected guts and organs and lay everything in a pile downhill from the animal's body. "For the coyotes and the crows," he said. He took up his bone saw again and sawed the pelvis into two halves and hand-scraped them clean.

Dave had come up behind him and stood watching him work. "Nice," he said. Doug glanced over his shoulder and saw both Dave and Roy standing there with Max between them, and he grinned at the sight of the three. He'd like to have a photo of that. "Pretty good timing," he said. "Not much for you to do now except help me carry out my pack and gun. I'm about done here." His hands were wet and bloody. He wiped his face and hands with his handkerchief and cleaned his knife and bone saw with snow and dried the knife blade and saw against his trousers.

Roy said, "Twelve points. He'll go one-seventy, one-eighty easy." Roy was a big man, as tall as Doug but one and a half times as heavy, a lover of tattoos with brightly colored lacy filigrees below his cuffs and rising above his collar to his ear lobes. "You gonna slouch pouch him or drag him out? Or quarter him and backpack him out?"

"I'll slouch him out. We can butcher him and divide the venison back at my place."

The other brother, Dave, shook his big bearded head. "You keep it all for now, Doug. We seen some tracks up above the kill even bigger than this old boy's. We'll chase him down and see you back at the house later." Dave was the oldest of the three, in his early forties, a slow talker, calm and complacent. He was the town road agent and was used to being in charge of men at work and treated family members the same way. He was a thick-bodied man, not as tall as Roy or Doug, and gave the impression of possessing great physical strength rarely called upon, like a retired athlete. He'd spent two years in the National Guard and served three tours in Iraq. Doug envied Dave for his military experience. He had avoided the Guard and Iraq and Afghanistan and was sorry he'd missed out on it. But when 9/11 happened and almost every eligible man in town had joined the military, he was still too young. He was already in love with Debbie and dreaming of marrying her as soon as it was legal. Then Debbie got pregnant with Max, and they did get married.

Doug was down on his knees sawing through the deer's leg bones below the dewclaws, leaving the hide still attached. "Watch, now," he said to Max. "This is how you make a slouch pouch."

Max said, "Why's it called a slouch pouch?"

Roy laughed and said, "Nobody except your dad calls it that. He made it up himself."

Doug took the strip of pelt dangling from the right front leg just above the dewclaw and tied it in a square knot to the strip dangling from the left rear leg, then did the same with the left front and right rear legs, so the strips crossed in the middle. Still on his knees, he swung around and leaned back against the warm body of the deer and drew the tied strips over his shoulders like the straps of a backpack.

"The hard part is standing up," he said and reached out with one hand.

Roy grabbed his hand and pulled him to a standing position, with the limp body of the deer wrapped around his back and shoulders as if clinging to him in a desperate, sad, parting embrace.

"I think we better get back to the house now," Doug said. "Zingerman for damn sure heard that shot."

Roy said, "C'mon, Doug, in for a dime, in for a dollar. We come this far, we might's well kill two deer as one. He'll be as pissed at us for taking one as he will for two."

Dave said, "No, Doug's right. We can come back another day. We can take that other buck when Zingerman's out of town. We can come back then."

They followed their own tracks out of the woods onto Zingerman's lane and hiked the quarter mile down the switch-backing gravel drive to where it met the town road. They all noted that the lane had been freshly plowed since they went in, but no one spoke of it, not even Max.

Zingerman's huge maroon Ford crew-cab pickup was parked facing them on the town road just beyond his property line, with Zingerman leaning against the shining, scoured blade of the plow, watching them approach. He wore a black military-style field jacket and a ski trooper's winter fur hat with the flaps drooping loosely like a hound dog's ears, and had what looked like an army-green Armalite AR-10 automatic rifle hooked to a wide canvas sling across his chest. It was not the type of gun you normally carried in your truck when you went out early to plow.

First came Roy with his rifle and backpack and then Dave, lugging his gun and pack and, slung over one shoulder, Doug's backpack, and behind Dave came Max, who carried his father's .30-06 with two hands, the barrel tilted against his shoulder like a crucifix. Bringing up the rear, bent from the weight of the slouch-pouched carcass of the gutted deer, came Doug, the last of the four to see Zingerman, the first to acknowledge it. He said, "Just walk on past him like it's normal. I'll do the talking for us."

When they were within a few feet of the property line, Zingerman spoke in that soft voice of his. "You boys stop right there," he said. "You're on my land."

They obeyed him, and everyone was silent. Finally Doug said, "Take Max to the house, guys. Yuri and I can discuss this together, right, Yuri?"

"No," he said. "No, we can't. We don't have anything to discuss. Don't anybody move, except to lay your guns on the ground. Even you, boy," he said to Max. He hadn't touched his own gun, which hung from his chest, except to caress it lightly with his fingertips.

Doug said, "Wait a minute now. Let these fellows and the boy go to the house, and you and I can discuss this little misunderstanding. I'm just trying to teach my son here his first real hunting lessons, that's all."

Zingerman unclipped his rifle from its sling and waved the barrel in the air in front of the three men and the boy, first at one, then the others, as if instructing them with a pointer. He said, "You three, lay your guns down, and then you can go. Doug, you stay put. You all understand that my land is legally posted, which means I caught you trespassing and poaching. Breaking the law, Doug. That should be your boy's first real hunting lesson, I'd say."

Doug said, "Go ahead, do as he says," and Dave and Roy and Max placed their rifles gently on the ground. "Go on to the house," he said. "I'll bring the guns."

Dave took Max by the hand, and he and Roy and Max stepped away from the rifles and crossed Zingerman's property line onto the town road and walked past his truck and stood together behind it, looking back at Zingerman and Doug.

"Now drop my deer in the truck bed, Doug."

"Wait a minute. It's not your deer. It's mine."

"No, it's my deer, Doug. You were trying to steal it from me. And I caught you."

"I shot it and gutted it and carried it out, and this winter me and my family are going to eat it."

Zingerman brought his gun barrel up and took a standing shooting position with the gun aimed at Doug's forehead.

Doug said, "Okay, it's your deer."

He walked to the back of Zingerman's pickup, and with

Zingerman's gun still aimed at his head, he dropped the tailgate and turned his back to the truck bed and slipped out of the fur straps and off-loaded the body of the deer. He pushed the carcass a short way into the bed and shoved the tailgate back into place. The deer was curled in on itself like a big brown dog sleeping by a fire. "Let me collect our guns, and we'll go home," he said.

"No. Leave the guns where they are. Go home now," Zingerman said.

"What?"

"You heard me. Go."

"No. Not without the guns."

"Doug, I can fucking shoot you dead and be within my rights. Now go home. Your guns will be here when I'm gone," he said. "And don't you or any of your family ever put a foot on my land again."

Doug nodded acceptance and backed slowly away and turned and slumped along behind his brothers-in-law and his son as far as his driveway, where the four of them stopped again and turned back like a family abandoned. They watched as Zingerman got into his pickup, started the engine, put it in gear and drove over the guns, crunching them against the frozen snow-covered ground. He put the truck in reverse and drove over them again, went forward and ground them into the gravel and snow a third time, and disappeared down his lane into the darkened woods and was gone.

When they retrieved their guns, the stocks and scopes of Doug's .30-06 and Dave's Remington 700 and Roy's beloved Winchester 63 were crushed and bent and pretty much beyond repair, certainly beyond cheap or easy repair, and none of the three knew anyone within a hundred miles who could fix them.

That all took place three years earlier. It was the last time Max, who was then eleven, went hunting with his father and uncles, who eventually replaced their guns with lesser rifles from Walmart and altered their annual deer season rituals by driving out of town to hunt on fallow or abandoned, uncultivated land owned by dairy farmers on the Lake Champlain floodplain, mostly open fields crisscrossed by creek-bed thatches of cottonwood and willow, land more suitable for bird hunting than for deer. They each found and shot a buck on those fields, easy shots, almost as if they were hunting semidomesticated deer on a game preserve.

But their deep woods deer-hunting days seemed to be over, unless they went on expeditionary hunts into the Adirondack Mountains or the Northeast Kingdom up near the Canadian border, which made them give over too many days and nights to justify the expense and work lost. It took a full day to drive there and hike into a borrowed campsite, two days or longer hunkered down in the shack or slabwood lean-to when not thrashing through the rough, mountainous, snow-covered terrain, and another full day to hike out and drive home. And when they actually did manage to kill a deer, hauling its body and all their camping gear and guns and leftover food and liquor five or six miles or more out of the wilderness to the truck they'd left in one of the DOT off-road parking lots, made it almost not worth the effort. It wasn't the kind of hunt Doug could share with Max, either. The men usually drank themselves drunk in the evenings and when bad weather kept them confined to the camp, telling lies and sexually sordid tales about themselves and men who weren't present and their women. Not something that Doug and especially Debbie wanted Max exposed to.

For those three years, until the Saturday morning when Doug finally went out to Zingerman's training facility to confront him about the shooting barrages, which is where this story began, there was no personal contact between the two men. There was quite a bit of impersonal, even legalistic contact, however, as Doug tried to close down Zingerman's shooting range—or training center or whatever it was—first, by appealing to the town select board, charging that Zingerman was operating a commercial business in an area that was not zoned for it. And when the board turned down his complaint and revised the zoning regulations to accommodate Zingerman, Doug went to the state tourist board, claiming that Zingerman was running a recreational facility without a license. The tourist board promptly issued Zingerman a license to run a recreational shooting range open to the general public. But the general public was never invited and never came. There continued to be dozens of out-of-state and downstate vehicles passing Doug and Debbie's house on their way to Zinger-

man's, especially on weekends, but people from the Sam
Dent region never seemed to go out there to practice their
shooting, no doubt put off by the Private Property and
No Trespassing and No Hunting signs and Zingerman's
less-than-welcoming attitude.

Finally, last summer Doug wrote a series of angry, florid
letters to the editor of the regional weekly newspaper, *The
Republican Register*, generating a variety of responses from
local folks, most of them in general sympathy with Doug's
outrage, though they didn't wholly share it, since only Doug
lived close enough to the firing range to hear the constant
waves of automatic gunfire and the explosions, and no one
felt as he did, that his ancestral lands and hunting grounds
had somehow been stolen from him.

By then he, and to a lesser extent Debbie, had become
obsessed with Zingerman's presence and activities and had
begun following him on his company website and Facebook
page and writing about him and republishing Doug's letters to *The Republican Register* on Debbie's Facebook page.
That's how the feud between Zingerman and Doug, at least
Doug's version of the feud, got known by hundreds and
then thousands of people who otherwise would never have
heard of either man. Zingerman himself didn't respond to
Doug's letters and postings one way or the other, until later.

All this took place before the Covid-19 virus pandemic
of 2020 and 2021, or things might have turned out differ-
ently. Or come to think of it, maybe not. Neither Doug's
nor Zingerman's character and priorities would have been
altered by the restrictions imposed on all of us by the pandemic. The two would have behaved exactly as in fact they

did behave, and Debbie and Max, too. We are who we are, and they believed they were who they were—even Max. If we don't find one way to hurt ourselves, we'll find another.

At first Doug's letters to the editor of *The Republican Register* complained about the gunfire and the occasional explosions coming from Zingerman's, as if he were merely and solely describing a noise nuisance. *We choose to live in the country so we can have peace and quiet, far from the bedlam of Gotham,* he wrote. *You don't expect the Joker to move in next door and open a shooting range and start blowing up old cars and attracting all kinds of gun-toting strangers who don't do anything to boost our local economy, since they eat and stay over at Mr. Zingerman's property like it's a B & B.* Trying for a little humor, he added, *Where is Batman when you need him?*

A few weeks later he wrote, *The liberal local politicians who sit on the Select Board and run this town have once again refused to act on a tax-paying citizen's complaint against a business operation that violates our democratically passed zoning regulations. Mr. Zingerman's operation is a commercial enterprise located illegally inside the Sam Dent residential zone, pure and simple. If it's not a commercial enterprise, legal or illegal, then maybe it's a training camp for political extremists or a private militia, as many of us suspect. In which case, where is the federal government when you need it? Busy pushing to get rid of the Second Amendment, I suppose, or defunding the police. So who's going to defend us ordinary citizens against these trigger-happy bomb-making extremists when they decide to overturn legitimate government with a coup or foment a race war? This country needs to get its priorities straight.*

Gradually, Doug's letters came to reflect his hardening view, confirmed by his and Debbie's scrutiny of Zingerman's website and Facebook page, that a training camp for militant extremists was operating openly in what used to be called Lafleur's Woods.

Throughout that summer, as he had for a decade and a half, Doug worked five and six days a week as a caretaker for the summer residents, fixing their broken faucets, cutting brush, splitting and stacking firewood for their custom-made brook-stone fireplaces, reshingling the roofs of their guest quarters, lugging their trash and recyclables to the town dump, through it all trying to feel less like a servant than a local woodsman helping inept city folks adapt to a rural environment. When he came home at the end of the day, he would often get out of his truck and lean back against the fender and look out at his father's and grandfather's forestland for a few moments and smoke a cigarette and try to regather and resolve his turbulent, tangled, conflicted emotions before going in to Debbie and the kids.

On the one hand, like nearly all his friends and neighbors, Doug was a dedicated Second Amendment man. He believed that a well-regulated militia was necessary for the security of a free state and that the constitutionally guaranteed and God-given right of the people to keep and bear arms shall not be infringed. If that's all Zingerman is trying to do, he thought, if all he wants is to establish a well-regulated, well-trained militia and defend his and their right to keep and bear arms, then Doug had no problem with the man. Except for the noise, which he had to admit, in the defense of the Second Amendment to the United States Constitution, was a small price to pay. He could deal with that, if he had to. In the last election he had voted for Donald Trump, after all, in order to protect those very rights, and he'd do it again, even though certain aspects of Trump's character surprised and offended him, and in the end had caused Debbie to vote for Hillary Clinton.

So it wasn't the guns and explosives that enraged him or even what he assumed were Zingerman's politics. In fact, if what the man claimed on his website was true—that after high school in New Jersey he had emigrated to Israel and joined the Israel Defense Forces and had risen in the Duvdevan and had been a member of the elite undercover counterterrorist Sayeret unit, as described on his website, learning and practicing skills and death-dealing tricks that he later brought back to help train Americans dedicated to protecting the American way of life—then the man had earned Doug's respect and admiration. Yuri Zingerman was one of the good guys, a patriot.

It was his particular, thwarting use of Doug's father's and grandfather's land that made Zingerman Doug's enemy. It felt of a piece with the many forms of oppression and discrimination that afflicted him and made him feel small, weak, and childlike, made him think of himself as dumb and ignorant. Somehow, Doug felt, Yuri Zingerman and his New Jersey–based security company and firing range were in cahoots with the bankers who had talked him into borrowing $50,000 at 6 percent interest over thirty years in order to have a home of his own, and the realtors who had urged him and his sisters to sell off their father's land to someone who would turn around and ban him and his sisters' husbands from hunting on the land, and the summer residents who paid him the minimum wage to do their bidding and treated him like their lackey, and the local and state politicians who sided with an out-of-state businessman against an ordinary local citizen, and the state and federal politicians who, except for President Trump, kept trying to take away his right to own firearms, all of whom he believed were secretly conspiring together to impoverish and humiliate him and keep him from being the man he was meant to be.

He tried several times to explain this to Debbie, but it was like a ball of snakes, and he couldn't separate the many strands of oppression and humiliation and identify their individual weaknesses and kill the snakes by cutting off their heads one by one and wake up one morning brimming with self-respect, a man among men admired by women and children and other men, a man able to walk into the Noonmark Diner or the Spread Eagle and sit and listen to people instead of talking nonsense to them, a man who nods his head in silence like a sage instead of singing folk tunes and playing the banjo like a clever monkey, a man who goes home after two drinks and lets other people in his absence tell stories of his calm prowess in the field and forests and praise his skills with hand tools and firearms passed from father to son and his dedication and competence in the management of his family and financial life, a man who could find the money and time to build his own two-vehicle garage with a tool shop attached.

Doug sat down in his place at the head of the table with Debbie opposite and the twins seated on one side and Max on the other. Debbie silenced the kids by thanking the Lord, as usual, for providing their macaroni and cheese and steamed broccoli, Amen.

Doug barked a small laugh and said, "Then we ought to thank the U.S. government for the food stamps, too."

"Doug, show a little respect."

When the kids began to eat, Debbie raised her fork to her mouth, and Doug stopped her there, her forkful of broccoli held in the air six inches from her open mouth, by saying, as if speculating about tonight's weather, "I've been wondering lately if it would make any difference to anyone, even you guys, if I put a bullet in my head." He hadn't planned to say it, he hadn't even thought it. He just opened his mouth and the words came tumbling out. He heard them for the first time and at the same instant as his family heard them, as if they'd been spoken by an invisible stranger seated at the table: *Would it make any difference to anyone, even you guys, if I put a bullet in my head?*

Max, his voice breaking, said, "Jeez, Dad. Jeez."

Lannie said to his twin sister, "What'd he say?"

Leanne said, "I dunno, I wasn't listening," and dug into her macaroni and cheese.

Debbie placed her fork on her plate and nailed him with her gray-eyed gaze. "Did you stop off at the Spread Eagle on the way home? You sound like it. Damn it, Doug. You sound like you've been there all afternoon."

"Don't start."

"Well, did you?"

"No."

"Don't lie to me, Doug. Not in front of the kids, anyhow."

"What, it's okay to lie if the kids aren't around?"

"That's what they call . . . what's it called? Passive-aggressive. I ask you a legitimate question, and you turn it into an accusation, so I end up defending my question. Jesus, Doug."

He tried to say he wasn't being what she called passive-aggressive, and he wasn't sure what she meant by it anyhow or why it was bad. "Where do you get this shit? From your church-lady friends?" He understood what his family had heard when he wondered aloud if it would make any difference to them if he shot himself, and as soon as he said it he was sorry he said it, especially in front of the kids. He hadn't meant to scare anyone, least of all his children. It was the sort of thing he should have saved for the end of the night, when he and Debbie were lying in bed and about to fall asleep, too tired and distracted and estranged by their separate minds to make love. In the dark he might have said it as a way to explain how painfully divided he felt toward Zingerman, whom he both envied and admired and whom he hated and mistrusted. That's what he should have done. It would have kept Debbie from being angry and suspicious and calling him passive-aggressive, and it would have kept the kids from being scared.

He reached out and laid his large hand over Max's little paw and smiled and said, "I was only kidding, Maxie. I just wanted you guys to show a little love, you know?"

Max looked down at his plate and in the voice of a much younger boy said, "That's okay. I knew you were only kidding."

Leanne said, "We love you, Daddy."

Lannie said, "Do I have to eat the broccoli?"

"Yes," Debbie said. "All of it."

As each of the next few deer hunting seasons came and went, Doug's obsession with Zingerman and his restricted use of the land thickened and grew. He became increasingly competent and thus confident on the computer, even though, unlike Debbie, who had taken secretarial courses in high school, his typing skills never advanced beyond pick-and-peck. On his own now, he tracked Zingerman's company website, ziptiesecurity.org, and personal Facebook page, usually checking in late at night after Debbie had gone to bed, feeling secretive about it and a little guilty, as if he were watching pornography.

One January night, after a few hours at the Spread Eagle, he came home, and when everyone had gone to bed, he went online and pulled his debit card from his wallet, thinking he might sign up for one of Zingerman's online courses. He was attracted to "Mastering Hotel Security for Soft Target Protection." It might qualify him for a job at one of the area ski resorts. Then he saw the price tag, $499.95. A week later, hoping to please Debbie, he got briefly interested in the "Israeli Security Training for Synagogues" course, $299.95, and clicked to see if there was one for protecting Catholic or even Protestant churches, but no.

By then Debbie seemed to have lost interest in Zingerman and regarded their neighbor as more of a nuisance than a danger, mostly because of the noise from the firearms and explosions, especially on weekends, though she worried a little about Doug's, to her, peculiar obsession with the man and what she called Zingerman's foreignness, by which she meant his being Jewish and from New Jersey. She did not believe she was anti-Semitic and told her friends at the St. Agnes Ladies' Aid Society that she was definitely not anti-Semitic. She said she was actually very impressed by Zingerman's having spent those years in the Holy Land as a volunteer member of an Israeli army anti-terrorist unit and wished that more young Christian men were willing to do the same. "Though it would've been neighborly of him to open his training center someplace else," she said and sighed. "It keeps us constantly on edge. Especially Doug."

Zingerman, on both his company website and Facebook page, had posted links and logos that were mysterious to Doug—digital doors he wasn't sure he wanted to open. But after a few months he worked up enough courage and curiosity to click on them, and he soon found himself staring at articles and photos and incomprehensible slogans that called for violent action against certain named politicians and Hollywood celebrities and other people whose names were vaguely familiar to him, authors and philosophers, he guessed, posted by groups and organizations he'd never heard of before, like Three Percenters and Oath Keepers and Proud Boys, plus some militia groups in other parts of the country promoting paramilitary training much like Zingerman's. He skimmed a few of the comments and chats posted on the groups' digital bulletin boards and hurriedly clicked off, as if he'd inadvertently stumbled onto a network of child pornography sites and feared being arrested for it.

The October morning when Debbie took the kids and drove into town with her Forester loaded with the thank-you-for-your-service boxes of wool caps, scarves, and mittens knitted by the ladies of St. Agnes for the men and women of the 10th Mountain 2nd Brigade in Afghanistan, Doug, left at home to his own devices, still nursing his hangover from the night before, sat down at the kitchen table and opened the family laptop and once again clicked his way to Zingerman's Facebook page.

Under the heading "Local Yokel Opposes Patriot Training in Yokel Newspaper" he read a pair of sentences that were embarrassingly familiar: *You don't expect the Joker to move in next door and open a shooting range and start blowing up old cars, attracting all kinds of gun-toting strangers who don't do anything to boost our local economy, since they eat and stay over at Mr. Zingerman's property like it's a B & B. Where is Batman when you need him?*

Below the heading, Facebook friends of Zingerman's, complete strangers to Doug, had written about Doug as if they knew him personally and hated him. They mocked him and listed the cruel and obscene punishments they wished to inflict on him and his family. One of them posted Doug's home address and cellphone number and provided a link to Google Maps that had pictures of the house taken from the driveway. There was a string of Twitter hashtags and more of those mysterious logos and links that he had stumbled onto earlier and had run away from.

When he clicked his shaken way back to Zingerman's main Facebook page, he recognized another of his sentences that had been posted during his seventeen-minute absence: *So who's going to defend us ordinary citizens against these trigger-happy bomb-making extremists when they decide to overturn legitimate government with a coup or foment a race war?* Then more mocking comments and Twitter threads and physical threats against Doug and his family. They wanted to rape Debbie and Leanne, castrate Doug and his sons, Max and Lannie, and burn down their house. As fast as he read one of these rants, another would appear on the screen. The texts and chats kept rolling in, overwriting and replacing themselves, as if the screen were alive and undulating and squirming its way closer and closer to him, opening its yawning, fanged mouth to swallow him whole.

Muttering to himself, he got up and walked rapidly from one room to the other, from the kitchen to the living room to the kids' cluttered bedroom to his and Debbie's bedroom, where he got down on his knees and looked under their unmade queen-sized bed and into their clothes closet, and went into the bathroom and yanked back the shower curtain and checked the tub, as if searching for evidence of the beast hiding inside the family home. He opened the jam-packed coat closet by the front door and circled back to the kitchen and went down the narrow stairs to the basement and prowled among the plywood worktables and bicycles and tricycles and his tool bench and the freezer and the rakes and snow shovels. Finally he exited the house by way of the cellar door to the bare, frozen backyard and circled the house, looking down at the frosted yellow grass near the windows for footprints or a spent shotgun shell or bullet casing or a dropped cigarette butt that wasn't one of his or Debbie's American Spirits.

Coatless and shivering, he checked his truck for signs of tampering, tires slashed or scratches from keying or spray-painted graffiti, and found none. He noted with relief that the Ruger rifle that he used for target practice and varmint shooting and for teaching Max how to shoot was still racked against the rear window of the cab. He'd carried the .22 with him yesterday to clear out a porcupine family's nest under the porch of one of the summer places he took care of and had forgotten to bring it inside when he got home from the Spread Eagle last night.

He climbed into the truck, got behind the wheel, and saw the keys dangling from the ignition. His memory of driving home and parking the truck and stumbling from the truck into the house was full of black holes eating the light. He must have been drunker than he thought when he pulled in, and he announced to himself once again that he would cut back on his drinking. Debbie's right, he said to himself, his drinking's getting out of hand.

He started the engine, popped the truck into reverse, backed quickly out of the driveway, spun the wheel, and stomped on the accelerator. Blasting past the Private Property, No Trespassing, No Hunting signs at the property line, he headed the truck into the woods. Doug hadn't crossed the line since Zingerman stole Doug's gutted deer and crushed Doug's and Roy's and Dave's precious hunting rifles three years ago. Rumbling over Blackstone Kill on Zingerman's bridge, he sped up the rising, switchbacked narrow lane past birch groves and black gum trees and oaks, ascending rapidly through pine and spruce forest, tires spitting clods of frozen gravel as he swerved through the bends and cuts in the rough corrugated lane, accelerating out of the curves and racing to the next, until he pulled up abruptly in front of Zingerman's chained and padlocked gate.

Next to him on the passenger seat he spotted the cherry-red Make America Great Again Trump campaign cap that had cost him eighteen dollars at Trump's Fort Pierce rally. The president and the Republican congresswoman for their district had flown in from Washington on Air Force One back in August to wave the 10th Mountain 2nd Brigade off to Afghanistan. After cruising the souvenir and food stands, he and Debbie had joined the crowd gathered on the tarmac and were making their way toward the stage when Doug disappeared. A few minutes later he returned wearing the MAGA cap. He grinned as if he'd gotten away with something. "You vote your way, I'll vote mine," he said.

She scowled and said, "It's got nothing to do with Trump. It's about the eighteen bucks that'll fill the gas tank, Doug."

"I'm just showing the colors, babe. Letting 'em know I'm not embarrassed for supporting the guy."

"Letting *who* know?"

"The libs and the snowflakes who pay me eighteen bucks for two hours' work splitting and stacking wood to make their living room fireplaces nice and cozy."

He put on the MAGA cap and stepped from the truck. An SUV with New Jersey plates and a rusted-out white pickup from New York were parked at the end of the circular driveway just beyond the gate. He looked around for Zingerman's Ford crew-cab truck and his Denali, but unless both vehicles were in the garage, the man he had come to deal with was gone.

The ground up here, his father's and grandfather's land, a thousand feet higher than his eight-acre yard below, was covered with crusted snow, and a cold wind seethed in the high branches of the surrounding pines. Zingerman's compound, carved out of the forest like a wilderness trading post, was surrounded by a six-foot-high metal fence. Set side by side in the probable order of their purchase and construction, a single-wide mobile home on cinderblocks was nearest the gate and behind it a bulbous, silver-and-black RV and then a three-bay windowless garage with a half dozen solar panels on the roof and a long, corrugated steel army surplus Quonset hut. Beyond the Quonset hut Doug could see a corner of the original slabwood hunting cabin that Zingerman had built shortly after buying the land, and beyond that the shooting range.

At the far side of the fenced area, a pair of large black-and-brown Rottweilers with heads shaped like anvils and orange agate eyes emerged almost sleepily from their separate doghouses and shambled across the snow-covered yard to the gate and stared at Doug through the bars. They curled their black lips back and flashed their teeth at him. They growled from the bottom of their wide chests, as if they weren't interested in wasting their energy to announce the presence of a stranger by barking or by running him off the property. They were attack dogs, not watchdogs, the kind that, if someone unchained the gate and released them, would pull Doug down and tear his flesh. Like a pair of hyenas, they'd break his bones for the marrow.

The front door of the single-wide swung open, and two men stepped out and stood on the landing. They were in their late forties or early fifties, one gaunt, the other beer-bellied, both wearing fleece vests over black T-shirts that advertised Zingerman's company, Zip-Tie Security, above the company logo, a bright green, three-pronged pitchfork. The scrawny one wore his thinning, coal-black hair in a stringy pigtail. The other, whose thick, gray-streaked beard

dribbled halfway down his chest, wore a camo MAGA cap
and appeared to have a shaved head under it. He was carrying an AK-47. Doug figured they worked for Zingerman,
hired out as bodyguards for New York City billionaires
or sports legends, probably. They were the Rottweilers'
human avatars.

Doug said, "I need to speak to Zingerman! To Yuri!" He
realized he was shouting. He lowered his voice and tried
again, "I need to speak to Yuri."

The one with the pigtail said, "Do you, now?"

"Yes."

The bearded man wearing the MAGA cap handed his
gun to the first man and stepped from the landing to the
ground and walked over to the gate and patted the dogs on
their steel foreheads. He said, "I like your cap, man."

"Thanks."

He pulled a key from his pocket and unlocked the padlock
on the chain. He held the gate closed with both hands and
let the loosened chain fall to the ground. "You a patriot?"

"Yeah. Sure."

"No, man. Are you a *patriot*?"

"Look, I just need to speak with Yuri." Doug started to
back away. It was obvious that Zingerman was not here.
Doug had nothing to say to these two. He saw that he was
swimming in dark waters.

The man glanced over at Doug's truck and turned back
to him and looked him up and down, as if visually frisk-
ing him for concealed weapons. "You, you're the guy from
down below. Lafleur, right?"

Doug didn't answer. He walked around the front of his
truck and opened the driver's-side door, but before he could

get behind the steering wheel, the bearded man had let the gate swing open, and the dogs silently rushed Doug, one racing around the front of the truck, the other behind it, as if trained for exactly this situation, reaching him together just as he managed to pull his legs back inside the cab. He tried to close the door against the dogs' big open-mouthed heads, but it was too late, and one of them caught his left pantleg at the cuff and the other clamped onto his right boot. The dogs were working as a team. Doug kicked at them with both feet, and when the pantleg started to rip and his boot was slipping off his foot, he reached behind him and pulled his Ruger off the rack. He lay the barrel across his left forearm, clamped his hand onto the steering wheel to steady the arm, and with his right hand flipped off the safety and fired twice straight into the faces of the dogs. He slammed the door shut and started the engine. As he spun the truck away from the fence, he saw the man with the pigtail slap a clip into the AK-47, but before the man could fire, Doug was swerving in a wide S out of the parking area, the wheels of his big Dodge Ram spinning, and then he was gone, and Zingerman's matched pair of Rottweilers lay bleeding on the crusted snow. The man wearing the MAGA cap had pulled out his cellphone and was punching in a call. The other man was struggling to release the clip jammed in his AK-47.

His heart still hammering, Doug barreled straight past his house out to Route 50, turned left, and drove into town.

He scanned the parking lots of the business district of the village, the Noonmark Diner and the IGA grocery store and the Stewart's convenience store and filling station and the Spread Eagle, looking for Zingerman's Denali or his Ford truck, all the while checking his rearview mirror for one of the vehicles he'd seen parked at Zingerman's encampment. He wasn't afraid of Zingerman's helpers coming after him. He wanted them to come for him. He hoped they would try to shoot him for killing Zingerman's dogs, so he could shoot them instead. They were sloppy and stupid and incompetent, and he believed that he was not.

He reached over for the Ruger .22 semiautomatic, and keeping one hand on the steering wheel, with the other refilled the ten-round magazine from the box of .22 longs he kept in the glove compartment. He cruised past the town hall, in case Zingerman had business with the town clerk or the select board or town manager. At the west end of town, he saw Debbie herding Max and the twins from the school playground and hustling them into her Forester. He quickly turned off the road onto Grist Mill Lane and parked by the side of the lane out of their sight and waited for her to drive away.

He hadn't rehearsed what he intended to say to Zingerman when he found him. He knew that as soon as he started to speak, the words would come. His body was bloated with rage and cold fear and a freshened feeling of righteousness that he trusted to create and drive the words. The attack by the dogs and his shooting them and escaping from Zingerman's men had only further inflamed him, making him feel more enraged, more frightened, more righteous than when he'd first read the postings and links on Zingerman's Facebook page and had gone looking for the man responsible with the sole intention of making him remove those ugly, mocking, threatening postings and links. He knew that if he spoke the words to himself now, his body would be calmed a little, and every time he framed his intended speech in his mind and said it to himself, his rage and fear and righteousness would diminish, until the flame in his chest flickered out and his nerves cooled and his righteous sense of superiority dissolved like salt in water, and by the time he met up with Zingerman he'd find himself apologizing for shooting the dogs and would show him his shredded pants and boot to justify it. He felt crazy, but he liked the feeling of craziness, and he didn't want to lose it and go back to being his old sane self.

He decided to drive home and nurture his craziness and let Zingerman come looking for him there. He didn't know it, but Zingerman was driving back to Sam Dent from the state capital, where he'd arranged to rent a booth at the upcoming gun show at the convention center and was about a half hour away, when the man wearing the MAGA cap, whose name was Leonard Lorraine, 53, a housepainter from Paterson, New Jersey, reached Zingerman in his Denali by cellphone. Lorraine told him what had been done to the dogs and offered to go after Doug with the other man, Arthur Furillo, 47, unemployed, from Saranac Lake, New York, and bring the sonofabitch back up to the Zip-Tie compound, and if the sonofabitch resisted, they'd put him down. "The same as he did the dogs," he said.

Zingerman calmly said he'd deal with Lafleur himself.

"Stand back and stand by," he told Lorraine. "We don't want any problems with the blue."

When Doug pulled into the driveway, Debbie's Forester was parked in its usual place. He grabbed his rifle and stepped gingerly down from the cab and looked at his torn pants and saw that his lower left leg was raked with long, deep, blood-seeping gouges and he was bleeding into his sock and boot. There was a puddle of blood on the floor of the truck. For the first time he felt the pain of his wounds. His other boot was punctured in a half dozen places and so was the foot inside. As the rush of adrenaline gradually dissipated, pain flooded both legs, and he realized that he couldn't walk. The dogs had likely torn the ligaments of his lower left leg and had broken bones in his right foot.

Clinging to the side of the truck bed with one hand and his rifle with the other, he worked his way around to the back of the truck and dropped the tailgate and placed the rifle down on the bed and hitched himself up onto the extended tailgate. He wanted to lie back in the bed of his truck and fall asleep there, and would have, but he was waiting for Zingerman to arrive. He planned to greet him sitting up with his gun laid across his lap.

Behind him, Debbie stepped from the kitchen onto the deck. She drew an unopened pack of cigarettes and her lighter from the pocket of her cargo pants and noticed that Doug's truck was back and he was seated on the tailgate, facing away from the house toward the lane. He was coatless, in shirtsleeves, and wearing that ridiculous MAGA hat that he bought last summer at the Fort Pierce Trump rally. He didn't appear to have heard her open and shut the sliding glass door to the kitchen. He seemed to be imagining for the hundredth time the two-vehicle garage with the workshop attached that he promised to build for her, if he could just figure out how to talk Ward Lumber into giving him a $25,000 line of credit. Or if he won the lottery, she thought. It was never going to get built, even she knew that. She decided it was unkind to keep complaining about it. She should just stop it. He was doing the best he could to support them, to hold on to what they had. She shouldn't keep asking for more.

She studied his lowered head and slumped shoulders. He must have driven to the Spread Eagle as soon as she and the kids left the house for what he liked to call his hangover cure, a tumbler of vodka with a few ounces of orange juice for color. She didn't want to nag him about the garage anymore, but she couldn't bear to hear his excuses and lies about his drinking and have to pretend to believe him. His lies made a liar out of her, too. Between her sympathy for Doug and her anger at his drinking, she no longer knew if she loved him or was just taking care of a weakened family member. The weakest member. Oh, Doug Lafleur, you poor bastard, she thought.

Max came out from the kitchen carrying a bowl of Fruit Loops. "We're out of milk," he said. "The twins used it all up."

"Put the cereal back and make yourself a baloney sandwich or something. It's lunchtime. I'll pick up some milk at the IGA later."

"What's Dad doing?"

"I dunno. G'wan inside, it's cold out here."

"You just don't want me to see you smoking," he said and turned to go in. "It's stupid."

"What's stupid?"

"You and Dad, pretending you don't smoke."

"We're not pretending. We're just . . ."

"What?"

"Nothing," she said, as Zingerman's long black Denali turned off Route 50 onto Lafleur Lane and pulled into the driveway behind Doug's truck.

"This should be interesting," Max said. "Dad's really pissed at him."

"You shouldn't be using that . . . that word," Debbie said, her voice trailing off. She and Max watched Zingerman get out of his car and walk slowly up to Doug. He was wearing a black leather jacket and his ski trooper's hat. Max and his mother were too far from the men to hear what they were saying.

With his legs apart and his hands loosely placed on his hips, Zingerman faced Doug for a few seconds, smiling slightly, as if bringing him good news. Suddenly he reached forward with both hands and yanked Doug to his feet. The rifle clattered to the ground, and Max saw that one of his father's pantlegs was shredded and the leg was bleeding.

"Mom, what's happening?"

"Oh my God!" she said and put the pack of cigarettes and lighter on the banister rail. She stepped down from the deck and ran toward the men. "Leave him alone!" she cried. "He's hurt! Can't you see he's hurt?"

Zingerman grabbed a fistful of Doug's shirtfront, sending his red MAGA cap flying, and with his free hand slapped him rapidly back and forth across the face and forehead, as if trying to wake a dead man.

Debbie shrieked, "Stop! Stop!" She clung to Zingerman's arm, and he shook her off like rainwater. Doug clawed feebly at Zingerman's face, but gravity was pulling him down a dark well, and he couldn't catch a handhold to stop his fall.

Max grabbed his father's rifle off the ground. The boy snapped off the safety and stepped away from the entangled adults. Zingerman saw him and released Doug, who slumped back onto the truck bed.

Debbie stepped between the two men and wrapped her arms around her husband, shielding him. She half turned and followed Zingerman's gaze and watched her son lift the barrel of the rifle. He shoved the stock against his shoulder and aimed at Zingerman. The Ruger is a light rifle, weighing less than four pounds, and the boy handled it with ease.

In that soft voice of his, Zingerman said, "You shouldn't play with guns, kid." His blue eyes were dry and impenetrable.

Max said, "I'm not playing. You get off my dad's land."

"You aren't gonna shoot anyone, son." He reached under his shirt in back, and his hand came out holding an automatic pistol. "I've watched kids your age blow themselves to bits in bus stations. They had a dead kid look. You don't have that dead kid look. They weren't afraid to die in order to kill," he said. "You are."

Debbie shrieked, "Put down the gun, Max! Put it down!"

Doug said, "It's all okay, Max. It's over. Put the gun down."

Zingerman took a step toward the boy, then another. He showed the boy his pistol, a Glock, as if it were a trophy. He didn't aim it at him—it was just something for the boy to be aware of. "Give me the rifle, son."

"I'm not your son." He waved the tip of the barrel at his father. "I'm his son."

"C'mon, give me the rifle," Zingerman said and extended a hand for it. "You're not gonna shoot anyone."

Max lowered the gun barrel, as if ready to turn the gun over to Zingerman, and then swung it back and aimed at Zingerman's chest, and he pulled the trigger, but not soon enough. Moving too fast to be located and observed, Max's target spun away from the line of fire like a diffracted electron and fired back, a head shot that killed the boy.

Debbie screamed—an animal dying alone in the forest. She let go of her husband and ran from the truck to her son and got down on her knees and cradled his destroyed head in her arms, moaning and weeping.

Doug lurched toward his son's crumpled body. Halfway there his legs gave out and he fell. He crawled to the boy and the boy's mother like a penitent, and he held the boy's hands in his own and whispered, "No, Max. No. No."

"Jesus Christ" was all Zingerman said. He slipped the Glock into its concealed waistband holster and walked back to his car, where he'd left his cellphone. He swung the driver's-side door open and reached in and unclipped the phone from the dashboard holder and tapped 9-1-1.

Through the windshield he saw Doug, seated on the ground, pick up the rifle. He saw the woman embrace and coo to the dead boy like a ground dove. Her face and hair and clothing were splashed with her son's blood. Doug half lay on the ground, holding the rifle like a man without hope trying to keep his family from being massacred.

Zingerman unsheathed his Glock again. The phone kept ringing and ringing and no one was picking up.

Doug lifted the gun and aimed it at Zingerman, who dropped the phone and simultaneously shifted into a shooting stance with the Glock in both hands and his elbows resting on the wide flat hood of the car.

Zingerman said, "Lafleur, you're a fucking dead man."

Doug said, "I'm a nowhere man." He tipped the barrel of the gun into his mouth as if it were a musical instrument, a clarinet or a saxophone.

Zingerman said, "Don't."

Debbie watched and said nothing. Her hands played with Max's collar, straightening it as if for a photograph.

Doug took the barrel of the gun out of his mouth and lay the rifle on the frozen ground. He turned to his son's body and embraced it and began to sob.

Zingerman reached down and picked up his cellphone. A dispatcher was on the line. "What's the nature of your emergency?" she asked.

He told her that a boy had been shot. "Send the police and an ambulance to the Lafleur residence on Lafleur Lane off Route 50. It's the only house there."

The county coroner's report stated that the 9-millimeter bullet from Zingerman's Glock caused considerable damage, passing from the entry point at a twenty-three-degree angle through the nasal cavity, the cerebellum and the top of the brain stem, where it exited the skull. The fourteen-year-old victim died when the brain stem ceased to function, which is to say he died instantly. Testimony from the parents of the deceased boy, who were witnesses to the shooting, confirmed that the person responsible for the boy's death had fired his gun in self-defense.

After the funeral at St. Agnes and the burial, Doug went into town only when necessary. He stopped drinking at the Spread Eagle. He avoided people he knew, even his sisters and brothers-in-law. Instead, he started spending his free time over at the Lake Monster bar in Port Henry, where no one knew the story of how his son had died, where no one knew that he had not taken up his gun and tried to kill the man who had shot his son.

He stopped showing up for work, and his clients began dropping him. Soon he had nothing but free time. Regis Warriner hired him at the Lake Monster as a daytime bartender, and after work he stayed on at the bar, drinking and telling stories and singing "Closing Time" at eleven. Driving his pickup back to Sam Dent one snowy night, he swerved off the road near Lincoln Pond and hit a tree and was killed.

Debbie put the house up for sale and moved back to town with her two remaining children and rented an apartment in a building owned by the manager of the IGA and went to work full time at the Noonmark. Yuri Zingerman bought the house and eight acres for its appraised value. Now he owns all the land once owned by Doug's father and grandfather and before that by the lumber barons and before that by the American colonists, the French, the Dutch, the Iroquois and Mi'kmaq, and before that by the animals alone.

The week after Zingerman closed on the purchase of Debbie and Doug's house, he brought in a bulldozer and demolished it. He pushed the wreckage into the cellar hole and topped it with soil from the ground nearby and let nature have its way with it. Before long the eight-acre lot was covered by young birch trees and a scattering of pines and was being absorbed by the forest. Deer could be seen from Route 50 grazing on the brush and tall grasses.

Zingerman shut down his business in New Jersey and now lives year-round on his compound in Sam Dent. He no longer provides security for celebrities and businessmen. He specializes instead in training men and women who wish to become skilled in martial arts and the use of automatic weapons and explosives for when it comes time to employ those skills in the restoration of America's God-given, constitutional rights and freedoms.

HOMESCHOOLING

THE STORY about the Weber family starts with a pair of identical houses built side by side one hundred fifty years ago on an east-facing, sloped meadow on a narrow dirt lane that's called High Street. It's an unpaved road, but people call it High Street because it looms above the town of Sam Dent like a green furrowed brow. Sam Dent is little more than a down-at-the-heels north country village now, but in the late 1800s it was a thriving industrial mill town clustered around two small shoe factories powered by a dam on the Blackstone Kill. The word *kill* is a Dutch word for "stream" and reminds us that the first nonnative settlers here, and thus the first landowners, surveyors, realtors, bankers, farmers, mill owners and workers, were Dutch, displaced later by the English, displaced in turn by the victorious Americans, some of whose descendants reside here today, along with summer residents from downstate and newcomers of various nationalities and races and ethnicities who have trickled in over the years. For all that, the year-round population, a bit more than one thousand, is about the same today as it was in the 1880s, when the twin houses were built on High Street.

Local legend has it that the owners of the shoe factories were first cousins, Dutchmen, both men named Herr. Their long-abandoned factories have since been converted and recycled over the years into a car repair shop, hardware store, pizza parlor, hair salon and, nowadays, tenement apartments. But the Victorian manses built on High Street by the factory owners, first by one Herr and a year later by his cousin, look and function more or less as they did when they were built. Each still serves as the primary residence of a local family that has made few visible alterations to the structures and outbuildings.

They are the largest private dwellings in town, Victorian stick-style piles of wood and slate with towers and gables and narrow, shuttered windows and wraparound porches and balustrades and an excess of gingerbread trim. They stand in striking, self-important contrast to the modest New England–style farmhouses and modern ranch and split-level homes and double- and single-wide mobile homes on small lots where the rest of the town's year-round residents live. The rooms are dark and high-ceilinged and expensive to heat. The plumbing, sewage, heating, and electrical systems are obsolete and in need of constant repair or replacement. In today's real estate market, houses like these do not move easily from For Sale to Sold.

Four years ago, when Kenneth and Barbara Odell arrived in Sam Dent, they were in their early thirties, and Kenneth had taken a junior administrative position at the Essex County Correctional Facility in Lewis, his first desk job since receiving his Master of Social Work degree from Utica University. The couple had met and married as undergraduates at the college. Their names, Ken and Barbie, amused their friends, for they somewhat resembled the famous dolls, though she was a brunette and he a blond. Once married, they took to calling each other Kenneth and Barbara, and their friends and family complied. Kenneth was advised by the prison authorities, for safety's sake, not to settle his young family close to the prison, so they shopped for their first house in several nearby towns, including Sam Dent, our town, seventeen miles southwest of the prison, where, as it happens, several of the guards also live.

Barbara loved the house on High Street at first sight. It had a country kitchen and a formal dining room and a living room with a fireplace. She envisioned dinner parties, her parents and college friends coming from downstate for weekends, separate bedrooms for each of their three children. It may have reminded her of the house in Utica where she grew up. She imagined the attached shed and carriage barn as safe places for the kids to play together on rainy days with their new friends from town, where they'd care for the animals housed there, rabbits and maybe a goat, a few chickens for fresh eggs. Or a donkey. "Yes, Kenneth, why not a donkey?"

Barbara had especially liked the way the house looked down onto the town from above. It was a pretty pastoral view and gave the viewer a slight feeling of separateness and superiority over the locals huddled in the valley below.

Kenneth saw only what was wrong with the house, but

that was his nature. It was in fair repair, but he suspected that the soft-spoken elderly accountant and his wife, who were selling their longtime home to retire to Florida, had likely exhausted themselves and their bank account maintaining it. Kenneth noticed gutters that needed replacing, cracked chimney crowns, sills starting to rot, wobbly porch posts and columns, missing panes and broken cames in the leaded stained-glass windows of the three-story tower. He saw loose slate shingles and siding, difficult and expensive to replace, and peeling exterior paint, and water-stained wallpaper in the living room. He noticed fifty-year-old plumbing fixtures and a wheezing hot-air furnace and rusting ductwork. Beyond that, he thought the Victorian style of the manse was a little pretentious, almost ugly. He intended to resist buying it, no matter what Barbara wanted. Even at the low price of $123,000.

But, as the realtor pointed out, except for the residents of the matching house a mere hundred yards away, they would have High Street and the broad, sloping, twenty-acre meadow that sprawled down to the Blackstone Kill valley and the village of Sam Dent all to themselves. That was a positive for both Kenneth and Barbara. They could plant a line of fast-growing white pines between the two houses, the realtor said. She mentioned that a very nice couple with four young adopted children lived next door.

Kenneth and Barbara wanted a cosmopolitan adult social life for themselves and neighborhood friends for their children, and they also wanted rural privacy. After the house tour, they sat in the realtor's car and compared notes, and Barbara said this house gave them all three. It was a place

where they could host and entertain their friends and rela-
tions from Utica and Syracuse, it was a socially healthy
environment for their children, and it gave them plenty
of privacy. The $25,000 down payment was coming as a
gift from Barbara's parents. The balance came from a pre-
approved loan from her parents' bank in Utica. As a result,
Barbara's preference counted for slightly more than Kenneth's. They agreed to make an offer of $105,000. They
ended settling with the retired accountant and his wife for
$110,000.

The closing took place in the realtor's home office in
downtown Sam Dent. When all the papers had been signed
and the check had passed from buyers to sellers, the four
stood and shook hands awkwardly, as if unsure what to
say or do next in order to end the ceremony. The portly
white-haired gentleman with his jolly, round wife had lived
in Kenneth's and Barbara's new house for more than thirty
years, and they had raised their children there.

The man said, "So I guess you don't mind living next
door to a pair of married lesbians and a bunch of colored
kids."

Kenneth said quickly, "No, no, of course not."

Barbara said, "Oh? They sound really interesting. We
look forward to getting to know them."

Kenneth wondered why he and Barbara hadn't asked the
realtor to tell them more about their High Street neighbors,
other than that they were a nice couple with four adopted
children. He and Barbara didn't want to seem prejudiced
or racist in any way, because they weren't. But it occurred
to him that, before agreeing to buy the house, maybe they

should have tried to learn a bit more about the people next door. Suddenly the distance between the two houses didn't seem as great as it had earlier.

"Yes, the Webers," the retired accountant continued. "Mis-sus and Mis-sus Weber. It's legal for homosexuals to marry now, you know. Two white women and four colored kids," he said. "Adopted from a state agency in Texas, I heard." The man's thin-lipped smile was like a lizard's. One almost expected a forked red tongue to flick between his lips. It was the triumphant, self-satisfied smile of a man who had pulled a fast one and now was free to reveal it to the victim.

The Odells didn't think of themselves as victims, however. They hoped to befriend the Weber mothers and their four Black children and were pleased that their own kids would have the opportunity to know children of another race, as Kenneth and Barbara hadn't yet seen anyone in the town who was not White. With a few noticeable exceptions, the only Black people living in Essex County—all of whom appeared to be young, most of them male, unmarried and probably transient adults—were the inmates serving time at the prison in Lewis where Kenneth worked.

A week after moving in, the Odells were still unpacking. It was early July, and they hadn't yet arranged for sending the kids to school and had met no one local, except the clerks at the IGA and hardware store and post office, and were feeling isolated and unknown in town. Barbara baked a batch of Toll House cookies and boxed a dozen of them nicely, tied the package with a blue ribbon, and placed it in the next-door neighbors' mailbox at the street, along with a card on which she'd written, "From your new neighbors, Kenneth and Barbara Odell. Enjoy!"

The following afternoon she strolled from the carriage barn down the long curled driveway to High Street and discovered in their own mailbox the same package tied with the same ribbon with all twelve Toll House cookies inside and a typed note that said, "Thank you, but we are strict vegans. Judith and Claire Weber."

When Kenneth arrived home from work, Barbara silently passed the note to him. She watched him read it while he ate one of the cookies. He said, "They're good. The cookies, I mean. Don't sweat it, they'll get eaten. The kids and I will eat them, for sure," he said and patted her shoulder. "What's that mean, they're 'strict vegans'? There's no meat in cookies, is there?"

"It's the milk and eggs, I guess. Vegans can't eat dairy products or eggs."

"Jesus, what *can* they eat? Is it some kind of allergy, d'you think?"

"No, no, it's the principle of the thing. No animal products, is all."

"What about leather belts and boots and gloves?" he asked, and pointed out that humans have been living off animals for a couple of hundred thousand years. Maybe longer. "So what 'principle of the thing' are we talking about here?"

"The principle of doing no harm to other living creatures, that's all."

"What harm is done to the cow that gives the milk or

the chicken that lays the egg?" Kenneth wanted to know. "They're only doing what comes naturally, right?"

Barbara didn't have an answer for him and didn't want to argue. She wasn't sure of the difference between a vegan and a vegetarian herself. But she secretly admired both. She had never met a fat vegan or vegetarian, they always looked fit and clear-eyed, and she respected their sensitivity to the feelings of animals, which, to some degree, she shared.

They still hadn't caught actual sight of their neighbors, even after several weeks. Throughout July and into August, the summer that year was unusually warm and balmy, one cloudless day after another, and Barbara and the children, Rita, Sam, and Delia, aged eight, seven, and five, spent most of their free time outside in the yard, the kids at play while Barbara, taking advantage of the fine weather, pruned back overgrown lilac and forsythia bushes and dug flower gardens lining the walk between the carriage barn and the side porch entry to the kitchen. Kenneth on weekends mowed the wide expansive lawn between the house and High Street seated on the big green John Deere mower he'd purchased at the local hardware store. Riding that mower across his front acreage, he felt like a farmer on his tractor plowing his fields, and he enjoyed the feeling. Barbara talked a lot about planting a vegetable garden next spring in the flat meadow over on the eastern side of the house, but not in the meadow in front, next to where the Webers had their abundantly overflowing garden. Not side by side with the Webers' bountiful plot. She made drawings of hers on grid paper and read seed catalogues.

They never in all that time caught a glimpse of the family next door. The Webers' life seemed to be lived entirely inside their house. Barbara and Kenneth did see their two dogs, however. Every morning, when Barbara came downstairs to the kitchen to fix breakfast for the kids—Kenneth would have already left for work—she'd glance out the window at the house next door and see the dogs, one of them coal black all over, the other white with brown spots, sniffing and peeing on the newly planted, knee-high pine tree border between the two properties. They looked like dogs from the animal shelter, glowering, pin-eyed, mid-sized pit bull mixes.

"Probably rescued from a dog-fighting ring," Kenneth said when she reported the sighting.

"That's a right thing to do," Barbara said. "Shelter dogs. Those poor animals."

Barbara instructed the kids not to approach the dogs until she and Daddy had a chance to be reassured by the Webers that it was safe. The next time she looked out the window, the dogs were gone, until evening, when they appeared again, sniffing and peeing on the frail little pine trees. She never saw anyone play with the animals or walk them on a leash or call them to come inside. The dogs just came out to the yard on their own and sniffed and peed and sometimes pooped, until, twice a day, bowlegged and chesty, with tails pronged like parentheses, they stomped back toward the house and went around the front porch to the far side, where the kitchen door was located, and disappeared.

Finally, in late August, after two months of inhabiting their new home, their first home, Kenneth and Barbara caught sight of their near neighbors. It was dusk on a Friday, a bit after six, and Kenneth, feeling sour and cynical after a hard day at the prison, was sitting on the side porch in one of their new Adirondack chairs with a glass of scotch and ice in hand, gazing across his private domain like a lord of the manor, letting his wasted rage at another day endured as a bureaucratic serf slowly dissipate and dissolve in the comfort of home, when Barbara, who had settled the kids for supper with a quick pot of macaroni and cheese, came out to join him. She carried her glass of Chardonnay and sat beside Kenneth and touched his hand gently. "Bad day, huh, babe?"

"Bad week." His new job left him feeling frustrated and unappreciated. His training and education and personal values were stuck at cross-purposes with the pragmatic and political priorities of the prison administration. Every time he brought forward some small initiative designed to improve the lives of the inmates and contribute to their social rehabilitation, it got shot down by the senior staff, often with ridicule and laughter. "Barbara, the only things they're interested in up there is control of the inmates. That and protecting their jobs and pensions."

That's when they saw the Weber family for the first time. They came around the front of their house from the far side, marching in single file, two White women at the head of the line and four Black children in descending order of height following behind—a tall girl who looked about twelve or thirteen, then a slender boy a few years younger, another girl of seven or eight, and an even younger boy, who walked with a noticeable limp, as if his right leg were paralyzed.

The children's faces were somber and intent and focused on the ground before them. They each carried a hoe or a rake or a shovel, and every few feet the group stopped, and one of the two women pointed to the ground, and a child with a rake or hoe drew something from the ground onto one of the shovels, and the child with the shovel deposited whatever it was into a black plastic garbage bag held open by the taller of the two mothers.

"What the hell are they doing?" Kenneth said.

"Cleaning up after the dogs, I think."

The women wore identical full-length dresses, pale brown and long-sleeved, buttoned to the throat and made from muslin or some other soft cloth. One of the two was unusually tall for a woman and broad-shouldered, the other smaller overall. Both were young and slim and, from this distance, attractive. They were bareheaded, apparently without makeup or lipstick or jewelry, and wore their long chestnut-colored hair in a Germanic, head-hugging braid. They appeared to be in their early or midthirties, like the Odells. The children were more conventionally dressed in jeans and cotton blouses and T-shirts and sneakers. The girls wore their hair in short pigtails tied with bright ribbons, and the boys' hair was cut close to the scalp. They were pretty, dark brown children and healthy looking—by Barbara's lights maybe a little thin—and extremely well-behaved, as they followed their mothers from one spot in the yard to the next and scooped up and bagged the droppings left by their dogs, for that is what they were doing.

"Do you think this has been going on all month, and we just never noticed?" Kenneth asked.

"What's been going on all month?"

"Cleaning up after the dogs."

"Not unless they've been doing it at night in the dark," Barbara said. "One of us would've seen them otherwise. Maybe they were doing it on the far side of the house, where we can't see them."

The group had arrived at the property line between the two houses and was working its way down the row of newly planted pine trees, where the dogs seemed to have made more frequent stops than anywhere else, marking off and claiming the limits of the Webers' realm and the beginning of the Odells'. Kenneth and Barbara thought it strange that the two women were dressed alike and wore their hair in that old-fashioned braid, as if they were nuns belonging to the same order.

Barbara said, "Do you think they're religious? I mean, like Amish or Mormons or something?"

"Could be," Kenneth said. The Odells weren't themselves religious. They thought of themselves as Protestant Christians and for the kids' sake planned to start attending the local Congregational church in the fall. Most of their social and political concerns aligned with the social and political concerns of the Trump administration and the conservative Republican congresswoman from their district and their personal friends from college and Barbara's parents. They had registered at the Town Hall as Independents, rather than Republicans or Democrats, but thought of themselves simply as conservatives. Because of their dislike of the Democrat candidate for president—as they saw it, Hillary Clinton was overly ambitious and thus could not

be trusted—in the recent election both Odells had voted for
Donald Trump, with reservations about what they called his
personal style. Kenneth claimed to vote "for the economy,"
by which he meant policies and programs that he believed
rich people supported. Barbara was against war and crime.

They had caught the women's eyes, and Kenneth raised
his hand in a slow, friendly wave, and the two waved back
in a way that seemed to the Odells not unfriendly, but
shy. The Weber children simply stared over at them and
at a word from one of the mothers returned to their work.
After a while the family seemed to have finished, and they
marched single file back the way they had come and disappeared from sight.

In the following weeks, as the Odells prepared their three
children for starting classes in September at the Sam Dent
elementary school, there were a few additional sightings
of the Webers and their children and their dogs. By Labor
Day the weather was sharply cooler. The late afternoon
light turned to hammered gold, and the leaves faded to a
paler shade of green and clicked dryly in the breeze, and
in the mornings a shimmering silver coat of frost covered
the lawn, and Kenneth no longer had to mow the grass. He
was talking of buying a used pickup with a plow so he could
keep their long driveway open over the winter and not have
to pay an unreliable local plowman to do it. He needed to
be able to get out early every morning and drive to work
and back, no matter the weather, he pointed out.

The Webers, too, seemed to be preparing for winter. The mothers were seen perched on ladders stapling sheets of clear plastic vinyl over the windows, while the children turned the soil and spread composted hay over their large, now-desiccated garden on their half of the twenty-acre field between High Street and the village below. Barbara planned to plant her garden in the spring, locating it on the hidden far side of the house, where it wouldn't compete with the Webers'. The possible comparison between their abundant garden and her first attempt at planting made her anxious. She had never grown her own vegetables before and didn't have help from four hard-working children, like the Weber women, and Kenneth had made it clear that he was not eager to plant and weed. That was not his job, he told her.

During a visit to the school principal's office to register Rita for third grade, Sam for second, and Delia for kinder-garten, Barbara mentioned to the principal, Ellen Shipley, that they had bought the house next door to the Weber family and wondered what time the school bus picked up and dropped off the Weber kids. The principal, a stout, freckled woman with graying blond hair cut short, said that the Weber children were homeschooled.

"Oh," Barbara said. "I was hoping they could ride the school bus together, our children and the Webers'. So they could help introduce our kids to the others." She paused for a few seconds. "The Weber mothers, they're qualified as teachers, then?"

Referring to the women, Judith and Claire, by their first names, Principal Shipley praised their pedagogical dili-gence and intelligence, and said that all four of their children, despite having come from what she called "a troubled home," scored higher on the standardized tests than the Sam Dent public school students of the same age. She said that Claire had run a private Christian preschool and kindergarten in Texas for years, and Judith used to be the school nurse here in Sam Dent. "They're more than qualified," she said.

"But wouldn't it be better for their children to attend public school? I mean, socially. Better for the local children, too," Barbara said, thinking of her three. "Especially since they're so bright and studious, I mean."

Principal Shipley tapped the eraser end of her pencil against the desk blotter as if signaling impatience with the question. She was a firmly seated, straight-backed person in her early fifties. She wasn't wearing a wedding ring, Barbara noticed, and wore a navy-blue blazer jacket and gray slacks and a white, open-collared tuxedo shirt. It occurred to Barbara that the principal might be a lesbian, too. Not that it mattered.

"Those poor kids have been through a lot of trauma, Mrs. Odell. A lot. They're going to need an abundance of time and hands-on mother-love in order to heal," she said. "Judith and Claire can provide both time and mother-love way better at home as a family than if their kids were attending school here in separate classes all day, every day."

"Trauma?" Barbara said. "They've been traumatized?"

"Yes. Judith and Claire wouldn't mind my telling you, especially since you're next-door neighbors. But it's no secret. They were taken from their drug-addicted mother by the state of Texas and placed in separate foster homes.

Judith and Claire took in all four, uniting them. The Texas Department of Family and Protective Services and the mother, a crack addict who was in prison, allowed Judith and Claire to legally adopt them and bring them here to live. Judith grew up here," she said. "The house has been in the Weber family for ages, and Judith and Claire, who's originally from Texas herself, had been living up there on High Street since Judith's parents died. So it's been good for everyone. They're a wonderful family, very loving, very self-sufficient. We're fortunate to have them in the community. You're fortunate to have them as neighbors, Mrs. Odell."

"Yes. Yes, we are. They've not been all that social, though."

"Well, they're very protective of their children, as you can imagine. Give them a little time," the principal said and smiled dismissively.

That same evening just before six, the kids had finished their supper, and Barbara and Kenneth were settling them in front of the TV to watch *SpongeBob SquarePants* in the room off the kitchen that had been the previous owner's woodshed, recycled by the Odells into a laundry and utility room that they called the playroom. The couple was ready to enjoy their evening cocktail before Kenneth made dinner for the grown-ups. Barbara and Kenneth Odell were creatures of routine and habit, and observed a partial but rigid distribution of labor. She was the cook, and he, who collected cookbooks, the chef. She made the kids' meals, he prepared theirs. When he and Barbara finished their dinner, she washed the dishes and pans, he put the kids to bed and read to them for thirty minutes. In the morning she woke the kids and made their breakfast. He woke earlier, made his own breakfast and lunch, and went to work at the prison in Lewis. On Sunday nights they wrote out their weekly menu jointly, and on Mondays she did the grocery shopping. She planted the flowers and shrubs and planned the vegetable garden. He mowed the grass. He was the breadwinner, she the housekeeper and nanny.

It was not exactly a prenuptial agreement, but they had organized their marriage in this manner from the beginning, when they were still in college, its structure based more on her parents' marriage than his, for he was the child of an alcoholic, single-parenting mother and barely knew his father. They rarely argued over the arrangement and had never renegotiated it, either. It seemed natural to both of them.

Drinks in hand, they were ready to adjourn to the living room, where Kenneth had set a crackling fire, when there was a knock on the kitchen porch door. They looked over and saw Judith Weber, the tall one, standing outside. She wore the same brown muslin dress as before, or one identical to it, and had wrapped her shoulders and covered her head in a dark green woolen shawl like a penitent. Kenneth swung open the door and with a sweep of his arm cordially invited her into the kitchen.

She clutched her shawl around her and shook her head no and said, "Ms. Odell, my wife and I would like to invite you and your children to come over tomorrow for tea, so we can all get to know each other. I'd invite you, too, Mr. Odell," she added, "but I expect you'll be at work then." She had bright blue eyes, very large and unblinking. All her other facial features, her taut, thin-lipped, unsmiling mouth, high cheekbones, narrow forehead, pale, unblemished skin, seemed organized around her eyes. It was difficult not to stare at them, even though they were impenetrable.

Barbara stammered a thank you and yes, she'd be delighted.

Judith said that Ellen Shipley, the school principal, had telephoned and urged her and Claire to meet with the Odells and introduce their children to the Odell children. "You made a good impression on Ellen. That's not easy. She's been very protective of our children."

Barbara was privately pleased to hear that she had made a good impression on the school principal. The woman had intimidated her slightly. They agreed to meet for tea the next day at four. For several minutes Barbara and Kenneth stood at the door and watched Judith, mission apparently accomplished, hurry back down the long curving driveway to the street, turn left by the mailbox, and cross to the Weber driveway and disappear on the far side of the house.

"That should be interesting," Kenneth said.

"What do you mean, 'interesting'?"

"Nothing, I guess. Just interesting. You know, to see if the houses are as alike inside as they are from the outside. Try to find out what they do for work," he said. "I'm curious. Neither of them seems to have a job."

"Oh, really, Kenneth, I can't ask them that. It feels . . . invasive," she said, and they carried their drinks into the living room and sat by the fire, and while they discussed

Barbara's visit to the school today, both silently wondered about their neighbors' source of income and calculated the costs of feeding and clothing four growing children and providing medical insurance and maintaining a house as large and old as theirs and heating it in winter, plus the local school and county property taxes and home and auto insurance and utilities, electricity and telephone and cable TV, if they had it. Kenneth figured they'd need at least $60,000 a year, $10,000 more than his salary, which was generously supplemented by another $20,000 per year from Barbara's parents, or the Odells themselves wouldn't be able to cover their own expenses.

The following afternoon at exactly four, Barbara led Rita, Sam, and Delia down the driveway to High Street, turned left, and walked along the unpaved lane for a hundred yards to the Weber driveway, the same route Judith had taken, and up the front path and around the front porch to the side porch of the house, where Judith and Claire awaited their arrival. Barbara introduced each of her children to the women, and as instructed earlier, Rita and Sam and even five-year-old Delia shook Judith's and Claire's extended hands and said, "Glad to meet you."

Judith's intense gaze held Barbara's attention again and almost kept her from looking at Claire, who was smaller and, by comparison, fragile-seeming. Claire had a strong, expressive voice, however, especially compared to Judith's thin monotone, and a slight southern accent, and she smiled warmly and invited the Odells into their house. "Welcome," she said. "Please come in and meet our children. They're very eager to know you all." As the three

Odell kids passed by her into the kitchen, she said to Delia, "I hope you like chocolate peanut-butter cookies, honey," and Delia said, "Yesss!" and pumped her little fist, which made the adults laugh, even Judith.

That evening, while their dinner awaited Kenneth's presentation and the kids watched another episode of *Sponge-Bob SquarePants*, Kenneth and Barbara adjourned as usual to the living room for their evening cocktail by the fire. Kenneth asked Barbara to give him the lowdown, as he called it, on her visit to the Webers.

She said there was no lowdown. The women were gracious and warmly welcoming, and provided vegan chocolate and peanut-butter cookies, which the kids loved as much as her own Toll House cookies. And, oh yes, herbal tea. The younger woman, Claire, shared the cookie recipe with Barbara, and she planned to make them tomorrow herself. The Weber children were polite and friendly and beautifully behaved, she told him, and the house was very well kept, everything neat and clean, if a little what she called "minimalist."

He asked what she meant by minimalist.

She said that the rooms had no more furniture or decoration than was essential, no paintings or framed photographs, other than pictures drawn in crayon by the children on sheets of paper pinned and taped to the walls and cabinets. No carpets or curtains, even. "It was like an old-fashioned schoolhouse," she said, and admitted it was a little . . . bare. But Judith and Claire seemed dedicated to raising their children in a healing environment, she added, using language that Kenneth did not believe was her own.

The children seemed intelligent and well-educated and very self-disciplined and definitely not religious, she said, at least not in the sense that Kenneth and Barbara had worried about. The two women were modest about the enterprise of raising four adopted Black children, she told him, and they spoke of it only indirectly and always in terms of the immediate needs of the children themselves. Not their own needs.

But what *were* Judith's and Claire's own needs? Kenneth wanted to know. And given those needs, how could he and Barbara know that the women weren't dangerous in some way? A danger to their adopted kids, he meant. He was concerned about the adopted kids, he said. As for not being religious, what about those monkish dresses and hairdos? Were they fundamentalist Christians? Maybe some weirdo evangelical, snake-handling, talking-in-tongues subgroup? Or bomb-building, Muslim fundamentalist terrorists? He was joking now. They could be one of those all-in, Bible-based Jewish groups, he told her, like Jews for Jesus. Or Hare Krishnas, like we used to see in airports with their shaved heads and begging bowls.

No, no, the Webers weren't deeply religious, not as far as she knew. In fact, they didn't seem to adhere to any particular religion. She thought their *beliefs* mattered more to them than their *ideas,* a distinction Kenneth found less than useful. It struck him as soft New Age spirituality rather than adherence to a formal religion, if he understood her meaning correctly, and said to himself that he did understand her meaning correctly, but he didn't say that aloud.

She meant only that they were ethical women, but not

because of any particular religious affiliation. She decided not to argue with him or explain her meaning. Something about the Weber women irritated Kenneth, and she didn't know what it was and wondered if he himself knew, and for that reason she did not want to confront him about it. Besides, if he didn't know why the women irritated him, he would just deny it.

The Webers' floor plan was exactly the same as the Odells', Barbara told him. It was slightly disorienting to be there, she said. Almost like dreaming it. The house was not as well maintained as theirs, she added, which wasn't true but she knew that's what he wanted to hear. Kenneth Odell was viewed by all who knew him as a peremptory and opinionated man, and, if not cynical, a man who was suspicious of other people's good intentions. But he judged others no more harshly than he judged himself, so she, like most of their friends and family members, rather than oppose him, let his opinions and judgments temper and slightly darken hers. Most people tend to tilt easily to the negative anyhow, and maybe every sentimental family or circle of friends needs a skeptic in its midst, and for that reason Barbara was easily seduced into bolstering her husband's skepticism, even when she did not share it. It helped keep things sweet and peaceful between them. But it meant that often, if she did not lie to herself, she lied to him, usually by omission.

For instance, she did not mention that there were no rugs or furniture in the living room, except for six ladder-back chairs with woven rush seats placed against the four walls facing each other. She did not tell him that there was no television in sight, no radio or CD player. The dining room was furnished with an eight-by-four-foot sheet of plywood set on sawhorses, nothing more. When it came time for cookies and milk, all the children stood around the sheet of plywood and ate in silence, which the Odell kids took in stride and did not seem to mind in the slightest. In fact, both Rita and Sam said later that it was fun to have your after-school snack standing up like at a counter in a cafe. While the children ate their cookies and drank their milk, the three women sat at the kitchen table and drank tea and amiably compared their plans for next summer's vegetable gardens. Barbara did not tell Kenneth that she learned more in an hour about what to plant and what not to plant in this particular climate zone and soil than she had learned from all the gardening books she had been studying over the summer.

Later, the Webers' four children were instructed by Judith to show their bedrooms upstairs to the Odell kids. Barbara did not tell Kenneth that Rita, the oldest of the Odell kids, reported that the two Weber boys shared one room and the two girls a second and were told by Anthea, the oldest of the Weber kids, not to peek into the other two bedrooms up there. Anthea told Rita that those were their mothers' separate bedrooms and no one was allowed to enter them except once a week to clean and dust and change the sheets. Anthea said that the kids did their school homework in their bedrooms at night and met for class together in the dining room during the day.

There was a bathroom up there, Rita reported to her mother, with an old-fashioned clawfoot tub and sink and a toilet that had a tank near the ceiling and a chain that you pulled to flush it. She said that when she told Anthea that she had to pee, the older girl said she would need permission from one of Anthea's mothers, but Rita was too embarrassed to ask a stranger, so while Anthea was leading the kids on the tour of their bedrooms, she ducked into the bathroom and used the toilet without permission. Rita said she liked Anthea's quiet, shy way of explaining things you didn't think to ask about.

Barbara did not tell Kenneth any of this, because she did not yet know what she herself thought of the Webers and the way they were raising their children. She had learned that when you tried to discuss something with Kenneth, if you did not already know what you thought about it, you would end up thinking about it the same as he did or else not thinking about it at all. She wanted to learn more about the Weber women and their children, but on her own, not with Kenneth's guidance. There was something clean and rational and purposeful about the two women and their unusual way of life, and Barbara almost envied them for it. They seemed free to invent and control their shared life in a way that she and Kenneth were not. But there was also something threatening and reckless about it, and that gave her serious pause.

"What about the dogs?" Kenneth asked.

"What about them?"

"Well, were they good dogs? You know, friendly and obedient."

"Oh, yes! They didn't bark once and slept through our entire visit. I barely noticed them."

"That's reassuring," he said. "I was a little worried about those dogs."

★

Down in the town of Sam Dent, Judith and Claire Weber were viewed by most residents as model citizens. They did not quarrel with the townspeople or complain to the local authorities or law enforcement about small encroachments on their autonomy and privacy. They paid their county and town taxes on the house on High Street on time and attended annual town meetings and shopped locally whenever possible. They were not politically outspoken or controversial in any discernible way, although it was assumed—because they were lesbians and therefore no doubt supported Democrat policies intended to protect and even favor the rights of same-sex couples—they were members of the liberal set in town, not a large segment of the population.

Nor was it uncommon in Essex County for children to be homeschooled, although usually it was for religious or medical reasons, not, as in the Webers' case, to ease the children's transition from a drug- and crime-damaged family to one that was drug free and socially responsible. Adopting those four Black children was seen as charitable and self-sacrificing. Some of us did wonder if the children would fit in here when they became adults. But they were not expected to become permanent residents of Sam Dent anyhow. People assumed that as adults they'd likely go back to Texas or some other place where they felt welcomed because of their race, rather than in spite of it.

Judith and Claire belonged to neither the Protestant nor the Catholic church in town, but due to their old-fashioned matching clothing, hair style, and comportment, most people, in the manner of the Odells, viewed them as religious in some vaguely defined but acceptable sense. They didn't need to know the details, and in fact did not want to know them. One's religion, like one's politics, was nobody's business but one's own, and it was obvious that the Webers' religious views were at the conservative end of the spectrum, and that was enough.

And it did not hurt that Judith Weber was the last living member of an old, respected Sam Dent family descended from the Herr cousin who had owned one of the original shoe factories on Blackstone Kill and had built the house on High Street where she and her wife and their adopted children now resided. Since neither woman, as far as anyone knew, held a paying job, it was thought that Judith must have inherited money along with the house. Nor did it hurt that Claire was pretty in a conventional, unsexy way and sweet and warm in a southern way and in Texas had operated a private Christian preschool and kindergarten. As for their being lesbians, most people viewed their sex life the way they viewed their religion—they didn't need to know the details. Nor did they particularly want to know them.

Besides, no one said they were lovers, and the two made no show of it by holding hands or nuzzling each other in public. Maybe they were simply female life-companions in what used to be called a Boston marriage and had gotten legally married so they could adopt and raise the four Black children together. Both women were without any other living family, as far as we knew, and given the government's

regulated health system and restrictive tax codes and pro-
bate laws, if they wanted to raise those four kids, it was no
doubt a legally and financially sound decision for them to
marry.

It was at first a little strange and discomfiting, however,
for folks to refer to them as wife and wife, instead of husband and wife. But over time it came to seem more or less
natural. Now, when Judith paid for her groceries at the IGA
and headed out to their big maroon Ford Explorer, Royce
Carter, the kid who ran the register, liked to call out, "Say
hi to your wife!" as if he were complimenting her somehow
for being married to a woman. It made him look tolerant
and broad-minded, without seeming cosmopolitan or elit-
ist, although Royce Carter would not have put it like that.

On the other hand, by shouting out the fact of their
marriage in public, Royce might have been mocking Judith
and Claire. Sometimes a compliment can function simultaneously as an insult. He may have been telling everyone in
earshot that he thought it was ridiculous for two women
to be married, that, legal or not, it was an aberrant arrangement and deserved to be pointed out and laughed at.

The thing that stood out for most folks, when it came
to Judith and Claire Weber, was not that they were lesbians and married, but that they had adopted four Black kids
from Texas whose mother had been a crack addict and was
in jail. In Sam Dent, race, as a meaningful social category,
trumped both lesbianism and same-sex marriage.

The Weber children were rarely seen in town, however,
except in the company of one or both of their mothers, who
kept them close and herded them like a small flock of docile

sheep. Even so, people were very conscious of their existence. Judith sometimes drove the family to the IGA and
purchased bags of trail mix and camp food. While she was
inside the store, Claire waited in the front passenger seat
and the four kids in back peered out the windows of the
maroon SUV like tourists on safari in an African country.
Judith brought the food out and got in the car and made
them put on their seatbelts and drove them out of town for
what people assumed were camping or hiking trips or in
winter a day of cross-country skiing at Mount Van Hoeven-
berg. Or maybe, as part of their homeschooling, they were
off on some sort of cultural expedition, a visit to the Hyde
Museum in Glens Falls or the Wild Center over in Tupper
Lake. There was always Ausable Chasm, good for a stroll
along the narrow catwalks slung from the sedimented cliffs
high above the rushing waters of the Ausable River and
Rainbow Falls below. Professors take Plattsburgh State students there to teach geology. Young kids love that place,
because it is truly scary, especially to adults who don't dare
to look down. And there was the Six Flags Great Escape
amusement park an hour's drive south in Queensbury,
where local folks liked to bring their kids on special occasions in the summer months, but it was difficult to imagine
the Webers taking their family there. Too cheaply commercial, too expensive. What it came down to is that most people didn't know where the Webers went on these outings.

So they argued over that. And they wondered where the
Webers got their money. And they speculated about the
ages of the children. They weren't used to assigning age
to Black kids. Neither Judith nor Claire volunteered that

sort of information, and people were reluctant to ask. They didn't want to be seen as prying or nosy. The school principal, Ellen Shipley, who was thought to be a friend of the Webers, probably knew how old they were, but folks were reluctant to ask her, too, unless they could claim a genuine need to know, and no one could.

All things considered, one could say that the Weber women and their children were easily and smoothly absorbed by the town. Despite that, to most of us they remained mysterious and alien. And not just to us. To the Odells, too, who were their next-door neighbors, who watched them come and go in their big maroon SUV and tend their garden and mow their lawn in summer and clean up after their dogs year-round and repair and paint the clapboards and slate shingles and wood shutters as they aged and weathered and cut and stack firewood in the fall and shovel snow in winter, and who, every few months, invited the Odells over to their house on High Street, briefly and formally for tea and cookies. Thus the Odells saw the Weber family more often and more intimately than anyone else in town, even including Ellen Shipley. Which is why later, when the official inquiry got under way, the authorities and the print and TV journalists interviewed Kenneth and Barbara Odell first and at greater length and more often than anyone else in town.

Following their first visit to the house next door, Barbara hand-wrote a polite thank-you note on her personal stationery. She added a PS: "Tell me when it would be possible for you and your children to visit us for tea and sample my poor attempt to duplicate Claire's delicious cookies," and placed the note in an envelope and put the envelope in the Webers' mailbox.

The next afternoon, when Barbara walked down the long driveway to the street, she found in the mailbox the August electric bill and Kenneth's weekly copy of *The Economist* and a folded sheet of paper, a typed, unsigned response to her invitation: "I'm sorry, but we are not yet able to let our children visit or play with other children except in their own home."

Puzzled and a little hurt, she decided not to show the note to Kenneth. She was afraid that somehow it would only heighten her anxiety about putting their three kids on a school bus for the first time tomorrow. "Turning them over to the care of the state," as Kenneth put it. There was no real connection between the Webers' rejection of her invitation and Rita's and Sam's and Delia's first day at a new school with a deluge of unknown, unstated rules and regulations and children and adults who all knew each other but were strangers to them. But it was hard for Barbara to disconnect the two situations, which she saw as essentially social and in conflict and somehow involving the Odells' three children and the Webers' four.

In her mind, that typed note had made a simple thing complicated. Her children had never ridden on a school bus before. She wondered if she should drive them to school, at least for this first day, or let them wait for the bus by the mailbox, as Ellen Shipley had suggested. Kenneth and

Barbara owned two cars. She could easily drop them off and pick them up in her Forester. In Utica they had lived close enough to the neighborhood elementary school for Rita and Sam to walk to class and back on their own. And Delia's private preschool based in a renovated carriage house on Genesee Street had been located across from Barbara's parents' home. If Barbara or Kenneth, who was still in grad school then and working nights as an attendant at the Mohawk Valley Psychiatric Center, couldn't pick Delia up after school, Barbara's mother or father could do it for them.

But what if it rains tomorrow? The poor things will be waiting in the rain for the bus to arrive. She wondered if the Sam Dent elementary school bus driver had been specially trained to drive the huge yellow vehicle carrying twenty or thirty hyperactive children in all kinds of weather on narrow country roads, some of them like High Street, unpaved. Should she wait by the mailbox with them in the morning or watch from the kitchen window?

What would Judith and Claire Weber do, she wondered, if they had to send their children off to public school? If they had to turn their four Black children over to the care of the state. There was a lot to be said for homeschooling, she said to herself. You always knew where your children were and that they were safe.

She dropped the Webers' note on the kitchen counter next to the electric bill and Kenneth's magazine and meant to throw it into the trash, but forgot. At the end of the day when Kenneth came in from work, he saw the note and stood by the counter and read it in silence, then looked at Barbara in an oddly accusatory way, as if she had done something wrong. He held the sheet of paper in front of him and read it aloud. " 'We are not yet able to let our children visit or play with other children except in their own home,' " he said. "Come on. Really?" He crumpled the note in his hand, walked into the living room and tossed it into the fireplace and silently set about laying the fire with kindling and newspaper. Barbara followed and stood at the door watching him.

Without looking up, he said, "These two girls, the Webers, they freak me out a little."

"They're not girls. They're grown women. They're our age. They're trying to do something good, something important that no one else is willing to do."

"And what is that, may I ask?"

"Save those children."

"From what?"

"From the state of Texas's foster care system, I guess."

"You don't know anything about that."

"And keeping them together as a family," she said.

"I don't know, it feels weird to me. It's like those kids are a hobby for them, the women. Or some kind of experiment. Like they're trying to prove something."

"And what would that be?" she asked, trying not to sound sarcastic.

"Oh, you know, that a couple of married lesbians can make a real family. Or that a pair of nice White liberal ladies can rescue a batch of poor Black children abandoned by their crackhead mother."

"Oh, please, Kenneth," she said and walked back to the kitchen to finish preparing supper for the kids.

Later that night, when they were in bed together, they talked more kindly to one another. She confessed that she was worried about the children riding the school bus for the first time and was anxious about how Rita and Sam would handle the difficulties of attending a new school and whether Delia would adapt to the longer hours of kindergarten after half days in preschool in Utica. And he admitted that he'd had a depressing day at the prison. Three of the guards had badly beaten one of the inmates, who was schizophrenic and should be in a mental hospital, not a maximum security prison, he told her. "Sometimes I wonder if I'm cut out for this," he said. Neither of them mentioned the Weber women or their children, and they fell asleep in each other's arms.

The following morning, Barbara delivered Rita, Sam, and Delia to the school bus. The windows of the bus were fogged over from the heat and breath of the two dozen children inside, and when the Odell kids had boarded the vehicle and the smiling middle-aged woman driver had cranked the door shut, Barbara could no longer see her children through the windows. She stood by the mailbox waving goodbye to them anyhow, until the bus had lumbered down High Street and turned toward the village and was finally out of sight.

In the afternoon, Barbara waited by the mailbox for close to a half hour before the bus finally delivered them back to her. Almost at once and without her asking, all three kids said they loved riding in the school bus.

"It was noisy, but it was fun," Sam said in his somber way. They claimed to like their teachers and had already made friends with kids in their respective grades whom they wanted to play with after school as soon as it could be arranged by the parents. They were tired and almost fell asleep during supper and had no interest in watching *SpongeBob SquarePants*, and after their baths went to bed without protesting.

That was during the first week of September, the Wednesday after Labor Day. Three more weeks passed, and the Odells settled into their new routines, and one evening after the kids had gone to bed and Barbara was clearing and washing the dishes and pans from their own dinner and Kenneth sat at the table reading *The Economist*, there was a soft knock at the door of the side porch.

It was a clear, cold, early October night, and a half moon drifted overhead, and strands of stars dangled across a black sky. The warm, brightly lit house, the kitchen and the living room and the playroom off the kitchen where the kids liked to lie on the carpeted floor and watch TV and the four bedrooms upstairs seemed like a mesh of protective cells, safe havens fortified against the coming cold and darkness beyond. The big old Victorian house, as summer ended and autumn replaced it and winter lurked in the near future, had become in a few short months a sanctuary for the family. This was American life in the country, and they liked it, all of them, the children as much as the parents. It had helped transform their family life into the center of the universe. It was a safe place of manageable size.

Kenneth stood and peered through the glass to see who

had knocked on their door this late. There was no stranger's car or truck in the driveway. Whoever had knocked on their door must have come on foot, which was odd, but not alarming. No one walks up at night unannounced, he thought. No one comes over from the village at nine-thirty to knock on the door of the Odell house on High Street. Unless there's an emergency. A car accident, a desperate need for a phone, a safe place for a woman escaping from her drunken husband, and he flashed for a second on his mother's fearful flights from his father before the old man finally moved out and left them alone in peace. He flicked on the porch light and saw a not very large person jump off the porch into the darkness.

Now he was alarmed. He pushed the door halfway open and shouted, "Who's out there?"

"Please, sir, please put out the light." It was a young male voice, thinned and withheld to just above a whisper.

"Who are you? What do you want?"

"It's Masai, sir. From next door."

"Oh. Well, come on in then," Kenneth said.

"Please put out the porch light, sir."

Barbara had come up behind Kenneth and peered over his shoulder. "Who is it?"

"One of the next-door kids, I think. He's hiding in the bushes. He wants me to put out the porch light."

She reached for the switch on the wall and shut off the overhead light, a simple, compliant gesture. "Come in," she said.

Kenneth backed away from the door and held it open for the boy, Masai, who was small, barely five feet tall, and dark and had a wide face and mouth and a large head and narrow neck and shoulders that made him seem oddly top-heavy, slightly out of balance. He darted from the bushes onto the porch and into the kitchen. Kenneth shut the door and turned to face him, arms crossed over his chest, as if to interrogate him rather than welcome him. These months of working at the prison had trained him in certain ways in how to talk to young Black men, although this was not a young man, he was a kid, a child, not quite an adolescent.

The boy stepped away from the porch window and stood against the wall by the stove. He wore a striped short-sleeved polo shirt and jeans and sneakers, no hat or coat against the cold. He was trembling and frightened, but it wasn't clear if he was more frightened of the Odells or of what or who had driven him from his home to theirs.

Kenneth said, "Masai? That's your name? Are you all right?"

Barbara said, "Would you like a cup of tea or milk? Are you hungry?"

He said, "Yes. Yes, ma'am, I'm very hungry."

Kenneth said, "You need to tell us why you came over here. And why you don't want to be seen here, Masai. So we can know how we can help you, if necessary."

Barbara placed a glass of milk and a small plate on the table with a pair of banana-nut muffins she'd baked that morning and waved at the chair for Masai to sit and eat and drink. He looked at the muffins and glass of milk for a long silent moment. The boy said to Kenneth, "I came to you because I'm so hungry, and my mothers won't let me have any food."

Barbara clapped both her hands against her chest and said, "Oh, dear God!"

The boy quickly sat at the table and began to eat the muffin as if he had not eaten in days. With the first muffin gone, he took several swallows of milk and proceeded to eat the second in three bites.

Kenneth said, "Why? Why won't they let you have any food?"

Masai looked up from his empty plate and said, "I did a bad thing. I broke some rules."

Kenneth said, "How old are you, Masai?"

"Sixteen."

Kenneth and Barbara were silent for a moment. They had thought he was much younger. He seemed so small and shy and afraid—how could he be a sixteen-year-old Black male? The child seated at the table did not match the picture in their minds.

"What rules did you break? I don't mean to pry," Barbara said. "I just need to know . . ."

He stared at the empty plate before him and didn't answer.

"Would you like something more to eat?" Barbara asked. "A sandwich, maybe? Peanut butter and jelly?"

"Yes, please," he said.

Kenneth said, "Your mothers don't know you're here, do they?"

"No. Probably not."

Barbara quickly made his sandwich and cut the crust off the bread the way her own kids liked their sandwiches and placed it on his plate, and he began to eat at once, as if afraid she would take it away before he finished.

Kenneth said, "Masai, I think your mothers will be upset and worried if they find you left the house without telling them. Maybe you should call them," he said and held out his cellphone.

"No! I should go back now." Masai pushed back the chair and moved toward the door.

Barbara said, "Where do they think you are? Right now."

"In the tower."

"The tower? Where's the tower?" she asked.

Kenneth answered for him. "You know, the same as ours, the third floor room off the attic with the windows all around it."

"But there's no heat up there. And no electricity," she said. "Unless they've renovated it."

"I suspect they have not renovated the attic room up there," Kenneth said. "The tower, good name for it."

Masai said, "Yes, it's very dark and cold. It's where we have to go when we've been bad or broke the rules. There's a little cot. And a chamber pot. They don't know I left, and if they find out they'll be mad. But I was getting really hungry."

"How long have you been confined to the tower?" Barbara asked.

"This was the third day."

"And nights, too?"

"Yes, ma'am."

"Without food and water?"

"There's a water jug for drinking."

"Oh, dear God, Masai, this is terrible! What on earth did you do to justify such a punishment?"

He looked up at the woman, his eyes filling with tears. "I got to go," he said and choked back a sob.

Kenneth said, "Masai, listen, we can call Child Protective Services. They can send someone to investigate."

"No! Don't call no one from the state! That'll only make things worse'n they already are. I'm sorry I bothered you," he said and edged toward the door. "Thank you for the food and the milk." He opened the door and stepped onto the porch, shut the door behind him, and darted into the darkness.

For a moment Kenneth and Barbara stared at each other in silence, trying to absorb what had just happened. Finally, she said, "That poor boy. What do you think he did that was so bad? I mean, to be punished that way?"

Kenneth said it didn't matter. If what the kid did was illegal, you bring in the authorities, the state police, and they deal with it as a crime. You do that whether it's your own kid or an adopted kid or whatever. The law's the law. The kid goes to juvenile court, and the judge decides on his punishment.

Or else it's some kind of private domestic issue. He broke one of their house rules. But in this case the punishment so far exceeds the crime that you start thinking child abuse. That's when you call in Child Protective Services, the CPS. You let them sort it out. That's what they're there for, he explained.

Kenneth was convinced that this was a case for the CPS, not the state police. He did not believe the boy had done anything illegal. Whatever rule he broke, it had to be a simple household rule. But confining him to an attic room without food or heat or electricity for three days and nights, that was definitely child abuse, he declared. Kenneth didn't care what the kid had done. As long as it wasn't a crime, he didn't deserve that degree of punishment. And even if it was a crime, no judge would clamp a sixteen-year-old in solitary for it and stop feeding him.

He believed the Webers were running their house like a prison instead of a home. "It's time to call in the CPS," he declared. "Let them conduct an official investigation into how those four kids are being treated. It might be much worse than anything you and I have imagined."

Barbara didn't agree. They didn't know if Masai was telling the truth, but even if he was, it might not be as punitive as it seems. He could be exaggerating, trying for undeserved sympathy. If the Child Protective Services got involved, they might decide, for trivial, unrelated reasons, as they often do, to break up the family unit and put the children into separate foster homes here in New York or ship them back into the Texas system, placing them with four different sets of foster parents again, people who would likely be taking them in solely for the money. That would be a disaster for those poor kids. The Weber women were undeniably eccentric, and they were homeschooling their adopted children, and therefore they could easily be judged as inadequate parents by an uptight, suspicious CPS investigator, especially since the Weber women were White and their children were Black.

"What does race have to do with it?" Kenneth wanted to know.

"A lot," she said, and reminded him of his belief that

Judith and Claire were conducting an experiment, that they were trying to prove that a pair of nice, White, liberal, married lesbians could rescue a batch of poor Black children abandoned by their crackhead mother and make a normal family with them.

He denied believing it. He was just speculating, he said. But he agreed not to call in the CPS investigators. At least not yet.

Meanwhile, Kenneth did a little research online and discovered that the Texas Department of Family and Protective Services paid $400 per month per child, or $545 for a child with "extraordinary needs," to qualified married couples who legally adopted children placed by the agency in foster homes. The child's birth parents, if alive, had to sign off on it, but most of the birth mothers and fathers, one or both, were incarcerated or had run off or were homeless and addicted and were almost relieved to let their children go, especially after being counseled by CPS psychologists.

Kenneth figured the Webers' smaller boy, the one with the limp, qualified as a child with extraordinary needs and thus was worth $545 a month. The other three together would bring in $1,200 a month, providing the Weber women with a total monthly stipend of $1,745. Add $949 worth of food stamps for a family of six from SNAP, the Supplemental Nutrition Assistance Program, and $1,000 from Obamacare to subsidize their medical insurance, and you have the taxpayers of the United States, Texas, and

New York paying the Weber women a minimum of $3,714 a month, $44,328 a year, to raise their four adopted children. There were probably still more federal and state assistance programs they were qualified to tap into as well, Kenneth thought. These women were smart and educated and obviously knew how to work the system.

A few days after Masai's surreptitious nighttime visit, while Barbara waited one afternoon by the mailbox for the school bus to deliver her children home, she caught sight of the Weber boy again. Evidently, he'd been released from the tower, his sentence either served or commuted. He was working outside in the vegetable garden with the other children, ripping up and composting the cornstalks, stripping the garden of the dead remains of the summer's bounty before the ground froze rock-hard. Barbara and Masai, barely fifty feet apart, stared at each other for a few seconds, but didn't speak or wave. She wondered if laboring in the fields was part of their homeschooling curriculum.

The boy said something Barbara couldn't hear to his older sister, Anthea—or maybe she wasn't older, just taller—and Anthea seemed to pass the word on to the younger two, the little girl and the lame boy whose names Barbara couldn't remember, and all four went diligently back to work. Though neither of the mothers was out there in the field to supervise them, they made Barbara think of the southern chain gangs of Black inmates alongside the highway clearing the gullies of kudzu that she'd seen as a child when every January her parents drove the family from Utica to Florida.

The two shovel-headed pit bull dogs, posted nearby like armed guards, seemed to have taken over Judith's and

Claire's supervisory roles. Then the school bus came rumbling up High Street, and she quickly put these thoughts
out of her mind.

Around this time folks in town gradually began turning
against the Webers. It wasn't because of anything new or
different that the Webers did or didn't do. But now that the
house next door, the Odells', had become the residence of
what was regarded as a normal, conventional, churchgoing
family of White people with a male father and a female
mother and three biological children who attended the
public school, the father employed by the prison system
and thus regarded as an officer of the law, the mother at
home keeping house and attending to the children's and
husband's domestic needs, it was almost as if folks had
decided that they were tired of being tolerant of the presence of the Weber women and their four Black children and
were no longer obliged to treat them as legitimate members of the community. The similarity of the Odells' and
the Webers' houses and the striking contrast between the
two families invited folks to choose between the two, and
they chose the Odells.

Even Ellen Shipley, the school principal, seemed to have
backed off her support of the Webers, as if her continuing
defense of them compromised her role as chief custodian
of the education of the children of the town. In the past
she had arranged to visit Judith's and Claire's house once
a month or so, ostensibly to see how the children were
advancing in their studies, in case the Webers eventually
decided to enroll them in the public system, and also to
socialize with the two women. Due to their sexual orienta-
tion and their refusal to join any of the many groups tied to

the religious, political, charitable, and educational organizations of the town, the pair seemed isolated and lonely on
their hill, and the principal had thought that she might be
uniquely positioned to soften their resistance to participat-
ing in the normal day-to-day life of the town. She felt sorry
for them and was afraid that they and their children were
growing increasingly alienated from the town, which was
not good for four adopted Black children from Texas. The
kids were her main concern, she explained.

But gradually she came to believe that Judith's and
Claire's alienation was self-inflicted and deliberate, and
that it had spread from them to their children like a virus,
and there was nothing she or anyone else in town could
say or do that would inoculate them against it. Reluctantly,
she had to let the Weber family go its own way, and she
gave up visiting them altogether. In a sense, Ellen Shipley,
like the rest of us, had chosen the town over Judith and
Claire Weber, even though, perhaps better than any of us,
she understood the reasons behind their willful alienation.
Later, of course, she would admit that their actions were
incomprehensible, even to her, who we believed had been
their only personal friend in town and who we assumed
was also a lesbian. It helped us realize that in the end what
Judith and Claire did had little, if anything, to do with their
being lesbians.

For the next month there was no sight of the Weber family
on High Street, except when Barbara and Kenneth twice

happened to see the SUV with the family aboard, Judith driving, departing early and returning late, evidently on a family outing or field trip. At the time, the Odells thought nothing of their neighbors' comings and goings, but folks later learned that credit card receipts placed the Webers on both occasions at the Ausable Chasm, where they had purchased four adult tickets at $32.95 each and two at $22.95 for children under twelve. So they were familiar with the place.

Ausable Chasm is called the Grand Canyon of the East, which is a bit of an exaggeration, but it is a spectacular, two-mile-long gorge hundreds of feet deep. The Ausable River roars between high, vertical, sedimented cliffs with narrow catwalks strung from the cliff walls overlooking the rushing, ice-cold water below. On his way to work and back Kenneth crossed the gorge daily on the two-lane Route 9 bridge and often glanced over the rail and down at the river hundreds of feet below, and he promised himself to take the family there in the spring.

Then, late one night in early November, weeks after the leaves had shed their autumn colors and had fallen to the ground and the bare trees were left behind like skeletons with blackened arms and fingers bent by the winds out of Canada, there came another soft knock at the kitchen porch door of the Odell house.

It was dark and overcast, no stars or moon. All the lights on the first floor of the house had been switched off. The children, Rita, Sam, and Delia, had long since gone to bed, and Barbara and Kenneth were in their bedroom upstairs reading, Barbara in bed and Kenneth stretched out on the chaise by the window. She was in her flannel nightgown, but Kenneth was still dressed. He asked if she'd heard a knock on the door downstairs, and she said it was probably a branch of a tree falling against the house. Then they heard it again. It was well past eleven o'clock. Someone was outside in the dark knocking quietly at their kitchen porch door.

Kenneth stood, walked to his side of the bed, opened the drawer of the bedside table, and took out his pistol. He released the trigger lock and snapped a fifteen-bullet magazine into the grip. It was a Glock 9mm, and he hadn't fired it since completing the New York Corrections Department training class in Utica a year ago.

Barbara said, "Kenneth, don't be ridiculous."

He ignored her and left the bedroom.

He walked through the darkened rooms downstairs without turning on any lights. In the kitchen, he stood with his back against the wall and reached over to the switch and flipped on the porch light. He looked out the window and saw no one on the porch or standing nearby. He swung open the door and moved into a firing position with the Glock extended chest high in both hands, his body turned slightly sideways, and said in what he hoped was a calm, authoritative voice, "Come out and show yourself!"

A child stepped forward from the darkness, a little Black girl with her hands up, palms facing the big White man with the gun. She appeared to be seven or eight years old and undernourished, wearing striped flannel pajamas and barefoot, and she was shivering from the cold.

"Oh, for heaven's sake, come inside," he said and lowered the gun. He turned on the kitchen overhead light, and the girl slipped into the kitchen. Like her brother Masai, she quickly dodged away from the window so as not to be seen from outside.

Barbara had put on her bathrobe and slippers and had come downstairs, and when she saw the girl she grabbed a lap robe from the back of the corner rocker and arranged it around the child's thin shoulders. She told her to sit in the chair while she made her some hot chocolate.

"Can I have some food?" she said. "Like you gave Masai."

Barbara said of course and made the child a peanut butter and jelly sandwich, not forgetting to cut off the crusts. She placed the sandwich on the girl's lap, and the child picked it up with both hands and devoured it almost at once. She had a dense thatch of hair that did not look cared for, and her dark brown skin was faded and ashen. Barbara took a carton of milk from the refrigerator and poured it into a saucepan and stood by the stove, heating the milk for the hot chocolate and watching the child finish off the sandwich.

"Would you like another?"

"Yes, ma'am."

Kenneth asked her name, and she said, "Arella . . . Arella Weber."

He tucked the pistol into his waistband and asked her what her name was before she was adopted, and she said, "Oh, Arella Harpswell. Emily Harpswell is my mother's name. My used-to-be mother, I mean."

He went into the playroom and came back with a pair of wool socks left in the boot cubby by one of his kids and kneeled down in front of the girl and started to slip the socks onto her bare feet. There were swollen, inflamed welts on the bottoms of her feet. He said, "How did you hurt your feet, Arella?"

"It's a allergy reaction," she said. "I'm allergic."

"Allergic to what? It looks like someone hit you on your feet with a stick or something. Did someone hit you?"

She shook her head no. Barbara brought her a mug of hot chocolate, and Arella sipped at it with her eyes tightly closed, as if to block the gaze of the man and woman standing over her.

"Have you been confined to the tower?" Kenneth asked, then rephrased it, "Do your mothers know you're here this late?"

She shook her head no.

Barbara caught Kenneth by the sleeve and led him from the kitchen into the dining room. She said, "We've got to do something to help this child. These children."

"What, kidnap them? No, we have to send her home. Tomorrow I'll call Child Protective Services," he said.

She nodded, and they returned to the kitchen together. As they passed the porch window, Kenneth glanced outside and saw the younger mother, Claire, step from the darkness onto the porch. She was wearing a navy watch cap and a bright blue ski jacket over her usual long brown dress and looked anxious and frightened. Her breath condensed in small clouds in front of her, and she was breathing hard, as if she'd been running.

Before she could knock, Kenneth swung open the door and blocked her entry. He was a large man, thick bodied, somewhat overweight and not athletic, but he took up a lot of space, and the woman couldn't see around him. He said, "Hello, Claire. It is Claire, right?"

"Yes, Claire. I'm sorry to bother you so late. Is my daughter here? Arella, is she here?"

"Has she run away?"

"No! Well, yes, she's easily upset. But it's just a family issue."

He said, "Well, she's here. But I'm worried about sending her home. She has injuries on her feet."

"You don't understand, Mr. Odell. These children, they've experienced a lot of horror. They've been brutalized and abandoned. I know you mean well, but you can't imagine what these children have been through, Mr. Odell."

"Yes, but the feet . . ."

"The children injure themselves. They lie. They're in profound emotional pain. They're bright and wonderful children, but they've experienced terrible violence and abuse. The truth is meaningless to them. They're feral, Mr. Odell. They will say anything to get what they want. Judith and I love them, and we're trying to save them from the effects of the violence they've endured. From the things they've witnessed. It's a terrible struggle," she said. "Please help us, Mr. Odell." And added, "Do not, do not hinder us."

Kenneth stepped aside and let her enter the kitchen. Arella sat in the corner rocker, the mug of hot chocolate clutched in her hands. Claire kneeled before the girl and embraced her bare legs, and Arella began to cry and said, "I'm sorry, Mommy." Then her voice changed, and she was no longer crying. She became calm and seductive. "You

want some hot chocolate, Mommy? Mrs. Odell makes wonderful hot chocolate. Here, try it," she said and held out
the mug.

Claire took the mug and sipped from it and agreed, it
was wonderful, and handed it back to her. "It's time for you
to run on home, honey. You should be in bed." Still kneel-
ing, she noticed the socks on Arella's feet and said to the
Odells, "I'll wash and return the socks tomorrow. Thank
you for loaning them to her."

She stood and faced Kenneth and Barbara and said that
she and her wife, Judith, appreciated their concern for the
children and apologized for any inconvenience they might
have caused. She told Arella to return home and go straight
back to bed. She'd be there in a minute to tuck her in.
She said she wanted to speak privately for a moment with
Mr. and Mrs. Odell, and the girl got up and walked out
the door and disappeared into the darkness between the
houses.

"The bottoms of her feet look like they've been struck by
something," Kenneth said.

"Yes, I know. As I said, they hurt themselves. They're
coping with a lot," she said in her soft Texas accent. "Eating disorders, nightmares, outbursts of violence. And they
lie, they lie with no purpose. I shouldn't be revealing these
things, but I want you to understand. You've been very
kind. But our children, they're like war refugees. They've
been traumatized beyond belief. They're suffering from a
kind of extreme PTSD. That's post traum—"

"I know what it is," Kenneth said.

"They're very bright," Claire continued. "But it's like
they're mentally ill, because of how they've been abused

and the terrible things they've witnessed. We're trying to nurse them back to health, so they can someday return to normal society and lead productive adult lives."

"So are you running some kind of mental hospital for kids, then?"

"We're a family, Mr. Odell. First and foremost, a loving family. But Judith and I, we're both trained to care for emotionally disturbed children. They need constancy and routine and discipline as much as they need food and shelter and schoolroom education. All of which we provide in ways that to someone outside might seem odd or unnecessary. We're trying to make it so they *won't* be committed to a mental hospital, Mr. Odell."

"So that's the reason for your matching dresses, yours and Judith's?" Barbara said. "A nurse's uniform, sort of, only not institutional white."

"Exactly."

"I get it," Barbara said.

"Thank you."

"I'm glad someone does," Kenneth said. "Are you and Judith licensed therapists?"

"Our children don't need therapy, Mr. Odell. They need love and order and security and instruction. And they need to live together as a family. As do we all," she said brightly and smiled. "No therapist can provide that. No government-run foster childcare system can, either. Only a loving family." She thanked them and apologized again and said goodnight. "I won't forget the socks," she said and stepped out to the porch and followed her daughter's path into the dark.

When she was gone from sight, Barbara said, "Well?"

Kenneth said, "I'll call Child Protective Services in the morning. Let them figure out what's true and what's not."

Which, as soon as he got to his office at the prison, he did. He called the 800 number listed for Child Protective Services in Essex County. The woman who answered was named Carol Evans, and to Kenneth she sounded Black, which he thought might be a good thing. He kept it formal and told Ms. Evans about apparent injuries and abuse to four Sam Dent siblings named Weber due to beatings, forced labor, punishment by isolation, and withholding food. He didn't mention their race.

He said that he and his wife had witnessed these things. He corrected himself: he and his wife hadn't actually witnessed these things being done to the children, but they had seen evidence of its having occurred or had been told about it by one or more of the children. To reinforce the veracity of his report, he said that he was a resident of Sam Dent and a state employee in the Department of Corrections. He and his wife wished to remain anonymous. He said that he was a neighbor with three children of his own, and they sometimes played with the Weber children.

Carol Evans, a calm, lawyerly woman, spoke to Kenneth as if they were colleagues, both in the same social-work business for the state of New York. She assured him that CPS was already aware of the Weber family in Sam Dent. They had been tasked by the Texas Department of Family and Protective Services to verify the presence in New York of Judith and Claire Weber and their four children, who had been adopted out of the Texas foster care program. Her office had already scheduled a visit to determine the level of care being provided with Texas state funds designated specifically for the benefit of the adopted children. They just hadn't gotten around to it yet.

"Too many cases," she said. "Not enough caseworkers. You know the problem, Kenneth," she said. She assured him that his call would put the case on a fast track. And not to worry, his identity would not be revealed to the Webers.

He asked her to report the results of their investigation back to him. Carol Evans hesitated, then said no, she couldn't do that. It would violate state regulations designed to protect the Webers' privacy. Unless, of course, the investigation resulted in bringing criminal charges against the Webers—child endangerment or fraudulent use of state funds, for example. A grand jury indictment would have to make the results of their department's investigation available to the public. She gave him her personal cell number and said to call her if he saw anything more that might affect their report.

"But a case like this, Kenneth, a married gay couple adopting four Black kids, it'd be red meat for the media," she said. "Especially social media like Facebook and Twitter. And you, an informer, an instigator? I mean, they'd be doxxed and trolled from both sides. But so would you, Kenneth. All you need is for one person to find out who blew the whistle, and they'd be on you and your family like hornets. You don't want that."

No, he certainly did not.

He suddenly regretted calling Child Protective Services at all and began to hope that when the CPS agents made their investigation they'd come up with nothing negative, certainly nothing criminal, and that would be the end of it.

We in town later learned—from the local and national TV and radio news as much as from the social media that Kenneth was so worried about—that sometime before Thanksgiving the CPS investigators did indeed visit the Weber home with their checklists and questionnaires, and they interviewed the children as well as the parents. According to the investigators' report, which was leaked either by someone at Essex County CPS or in the Texas Department of Family and Protective Services to Twitter and Facebook, the Weber children, two girls and two boys, were well cared for, clean and properly clothed. The house was set up with classrooms like a childcare center, the report stated, with separate bedrooms for girls and boys. The children seemed slightly malnourished, but the parents, Judith and Claire Weber, a married couple, claimed the children were still recovering from having been deprived of nutritious food while in foster homes in Texas. They showed no signs of physical mistreatment and spoke warmly about their adoptive parents. No further action was recommended.

It was unclear whether whoever leaked the report did so to enhance the reputation of the Weber family or to attack the trustworthiness of the state social service, because almost immediately people who read it took one of two opposite positions. Either the report erased hesitant, local suspicions that the Weber women were members of a religious cult mistreating their adopted children, or it confirmed suspicions that the liberal social-service agencies of New York were covering up a blatant case of child abuse, probably of a sexual nature, in an attempt to advance what was called the Weber women's homosexual agenda. Depending on their political predilections, people came down hard on one side or the other.

Except for Kenneth and Barbara Odell. The Odells knew too much, but not enough, of what went on next door to accept the blandly upbeat reassurance of the CPS report. Nor did they believe that a cabal of libertine liberals was secretly embedded deep in the state to advance the sexual abuse of children and promote by bureaucratic means the so-called homosexual agenda. So they remained unsure as to what was true and what wasn't.

They celebrated Thanksgiving with Barbara's parents and her sisters' families in Utica, and on their way back to Sam Dent the first snow started to fall, as it usually does late in November, but it was light and fell in thick wet flakes and didn't hamper their drive. Kenneth had bought by then a used seven-year-old Ford pickup with a plow and snow tires and chains and was looking forward to using it. At dusk when they pulled into the driveway, the house on High Street looked like a Christmas card. First Barbara said it admiringly, "It looks like a Christmas card." Then Kenneth said it wistfully, and each of the kids repeated it mockingly, and everyone was laughing when they got out of the car. By morning the snow was gone, and Kenneth's truck and plow stayed parked in the carriage barn.

Then, midway through the first week of December, an old-fashioned nor'easter moved up the East Coast and ran into a cold front off Maine. Kenneth squeezed their two cars into the carriage barn next to his pickup and waited for the storm to hit. The front backed in overnight and clobbered the region with high winds and by noon the following day had dumped nearly two feet of drifting snow on us. School was canceled, and Kenneth called the prison to say he couldn't get out. The line of tiny pines between the two houses was buried, and beyond the now-invisible border, behind the thick curtain of falling snow, the Weber house itself had faded from view, and for the first time Kenneth and Barbara and their kids felt like the only residents on High Street, isolated from the town and the world at large, but secure and happy together in their familial stronghold. It was almost as if the Webers during the night had moved out of their house and migrated back to Texas, leaving the Odells alone on their own hillside.

Around three that afternoon, the storm center cut back to the east, and the snow let up a bit. Kenneth put on his parka and boots and walked from the kitchen through the playroom and connecting shed to the carriage barn and started the pickup and went to work plowing the driveway, figuring he'd have to do it again at least once and probably twice before the storm ended. Barbara and the kids suited up in hats, mittens, boots, and parkas, and with brooms and brushes and shovels cleared the path from the driveway to the side porch steps, and when they had finished, while Dad drove his plow up and down the long curved driveway, Mom went inside to prepare supper, and the kids tumbled and played in the snow like bear cubs.

Two weeks before winter solstice, nightfall arrives in the

afternoon, and at four it starts to get dark. Kenneth switched on the headlights of his pickup and finished clearing the area where the driveway met the road. The town plows had not yet gotten to High Street, though he could see in the valley below the huge dump trucks passing along the main road, their high, wide plows in front and salt spreaders in back, their yellow roof lights flashing like beacons.

And then it was dark. It had started snowing heavily again. Kenneth the plowman decided it would be neighborly to clear the Webers' driveway for them, just one quick run to the turnaround by the porch and back down to High Street, so that in an emergency, once the town plow truck went through, the Webers could get out.

He put the pickup into gear, lowered the plow, and swept along High Street to the entrance of the Webers' driveway. It was buried beneath two feet of drifted snow, but its length and curve matched the Odells' driveway, so he knew where to plow without scalping the frozen yard beside it. He turned left from the street onto the driveway and slowly drove up to the turnaround by the wide sliding door of the carriage barn. The Webers must have parked their SUV inside. It was not in the driveway. As he approached, he noticed that the barn door was open a few inches, and then, after he made the turn, the door opened wider, and he saw two of the Weber children looking out. He thought it was Anthea and Masai, the two eldest. Then he realized all four were inside the barn peering out at him.

He stopped the truck and turned around in the seat and looked out the rear window of the cab. The four children were running from the barn toward his truck, each carrying a small backpack. They wore rubber garden boots and jeans, caps and light jackets. Anthea led the smallest of the four, the boy with the limp, who struggled to keep up, and Masai held his younger sister Arella by the hand. They reached the passenger side of the pickup and tossed their backpacks into the truck bed. Anthea wrenched open the door, and the four children piled into the cab. Anthea seated Arella on her lap. Masai, next to her, did the same with his tiny brother. Kenneth looked across at the four with shock and dismay. He was stunned and had no idea what to do or say.

Anthea said, "Go, go! Drive!"

Masai said, "Hurry up, mister, or they gonna catch us!"

The two dogs circled the truck barking ferociously, clambering against the doors of the cab and scratching the metal with their claws. Kenneth said, "Who? Who's gonna catch you? The dogs? Are you scared of the dogs?"

Anthea said, "Yes, them bad dogs, they gonna bite us! Go on, drive away from here! Please, mister!"

Kenneth lifted the plow, put the truck in gear, and drove rapidly back down the driveway where he'd already plowed, turned right onto High Street, drove the hundred yards to his own driveway, turned right again, and pulled up in front of the closed door of the carriage barn. The dogs did not seem to have followed them. He got out of the truck and shoved the heavy sliding door along its track, opening the darkened barn, and returned to the truck and drove it inside and shut off the engine. He got out again and flipped on the switch of the overhead light and pulled the huge door shut.

He turned around, and the four children had also gotten

out of the truck. They had retrieved their backpacks from the truck bed and were standing before him, shivering from the cold, looking up at him expectantly, as if waiting for him to tell them what was next, as if he had become their leader, their protector.

"Come in," he said. "Come in and get warm, and we'll figure this out."

In the kitchen, everyone in the Odell family, Kenneth, Barbara, and their three kids, hesitant and careful, but clearly with good intent, stood in a line to greet the four Weber children. The Odells wanted to help the children, refugees who had made the kind of escape the Odells had only heard about on television. It was as if the four had managed to flee to safety from ISIS or a Colombian drug cartel or a crazed middle-aged California couple living in a van.

Barbara and Kenneth and their kids, each in her and his own way, asked the Weber children if they were running away from home, had they had been mistreated, were they afraid of returning home, and where did they want to go? Back to Texas? To their foster parents? To some other family members they might have there? Kenneth asked if they wanted to turn themselves over to the New York Child Protective Services. Barbara asked if she could make them something to eat. Macaroni and cheese, perhaps. Delia asked, Would they like to watch television? Sam asked if they were cold. Would they like to borrow some sweaters? Rita, their eldest child, just watched, trying to think of a way she could help, but she was slightly intimidated by the two older Weber children, Anthea and Masai, and couldn't come up with anything. In her mind, the two knew more about the nature of the adult world than she would ever know.

The four escapees, with lowered heads and showing signs of shame and confusion, although they may not have been in the slightest ashamed or confused, deflected the Odells' questions and led them in circles away from simple answers. In a thin, high-pitched voice the youngest of the four said that his name was Royale, and he wished they could live in this house because it was so nice and warm and smelled so good. And they had television. "Do you get cable?" he asked through gapped teeth.

"We get all kinds of channels!" Delia said. "Like, hundreds."

The younger of the two Weber girls, Arella, a child with a clever smile, said, "We don't got no TV to watch. The mothers, they the only ones can watch," she added without breaking her smile.

Barbara asked her name, and she said it was Arella and spelled it for her. "I already told you before. Remember?"

"Yes, I remember now. How old are you, sweetheart?"

"Nine and a half," Arella said.

"And Royale, how old are you?" Barbara asked.

He looked at his sisters and his brother, as if he wasn't sure, and Anthea held up the five fingers of one hand and two of the other. He said, "Seven! Seven years old. Pretty soon I'm gonna be twelve. Right?" he said to his siblings, and they all nodded, and he smiled with satisfaction. He was the smallest of the four by far and dragged his right foot sideways behind the other, as if it had been attached incorrectly at birth. He looked younger than seven and acted even younger—but, yes, poor child, pretty soon he was going to be twelve.

That is the moment when the mothers, Judith and Claire Weber, appeared at the porch door. Kenneth told Barbara to get all the kids out of the kitchen, move them into the living room, he'll handle this.

Waving her arms like a hen flapping her wings, Barbara herded all seven children away from the porch window, down the hall and through the dining room into the living room where, earlier, while Kenneth was outside plowing, she had laid a fire in the fireplace. The fire was crackling nicely now.

Out on the porch, the Weber women in matching sky-blue ski jackets and knit caps were stamping the snow off their boots and brushing it off their shoulders. Their faces were twisted in conflicted expressions of anger and fear—a combustible mixture. Kenneth swung the porch door open and with his large body filled the doorway as much as he could. He stared at the women, as if waiting for them to state the reason for their presence, and they stared back at him, as if waiting for him to explain the presence of their children in his house. No one spoke. The silent standoff seemed to go on for several minutes.

Finally Judith said, "You have taken our children."

"No, they came to us on their own."

Claire stepped in front of Judith, her face red and knotted, teeth bared, suddenly the fiercer of the pair. "You and your wife have kidnapped our children!"

"No, we—"

Claire cut him off. "You fucking kidnapped our children! We're taking them back, you hear? Where have you put them?" she said, and pushed past Kenneth into the kitchen.

He turned around, and suddenly Judith was in the room, too. She said, "Claire, be cool! We can talk this out, can't we, Mr. Odell?"

Kenneth stepped in front of Claire to keep her from leaving the kitchen in search of her children, and the woman glared up at him, fists clenched as if she were about to punch him. Judith came up behind her and pulled her away.

Kenneth said, "These kids, they need to be protected from you two. I don't know why you adopted them in the first place, the two of you. If it was some kind of experiment or you wanted to prove something to the rest of the world or just to make yourselves feel good about yourselves. Maybe you did it for the money. But regardless, it's obvious you're abusing them. And it's obvious they want to get away from you."

Judith suddenly lost her composure, too, and she shouted at him that he had no right to judge them, none. Who did he think he was, questioning their motives for loving their children, accusing them of child abuse when he had nothing to go on except the complaints and lies of a sad group of children who were mentally ill? Who was he to judge them?

Now Claire became the calming influence. She put her face close to Judith's and tried to soothe her, backing her with her hands on her shoulders away from Kenneth, telling her to let it go, just get the kids and go home. "Fuck these people," she said. "They don't matter."

Kenneth said that he couldn't legally stop them from taking back their legally adopted children, but he told them that as soon as they walked out the door with the children, he was calling Child Protective Services to come and remove these poor abused kids from their custody. "I happen to know Carol Evans over there, and she gave me her personal phone number. She told me to call her if there was anything new to report on you two. And now there's plenty to report. Once these kids feel safe from you, once you're no longer able to intimidate and control them, believe me, they'll have lots to tell the CPS authorities. You'll be lucky if you ever get to see them again."

"You bastard," Claire said between gritted teeth. "You fucking racist asshole. People like you and your ass-licking wife are what's wrong with this world. We're not going to let you ruin our lives and the lives of our children."

Judith said, "Just give us back our children, and we'll leave peacefully. Maybe we can meet tomorrow, the four of us. Without the children present. Maybe we can discuss this calmly tomorrow and get over it."

Claire snarled, "There's nothing to discuss with these bastards."

Kenneth said, "Okay, wait here. I'll bring your kids to you."

He entered the living room, and Barbara and all seven children backed away from him, as if he were about to turn them over to the police. Kenneth said to the four Black children, "I'm sorry. You have to go home with your mothers. You can't stay here without their permission. It's the law. But don't worry, I'm calling in Child Protective Services, and they'll fix it so you can leave those women legally. You won't have to run away. You're too young to be on your own, anyhow. CPS will place you with good, loving foster homes," he said. "Who knows, maybe we could be your foster parents ourselves," he added, and Barbara stared at him in astonished disbelief, and Rita and Sam and Delia Odell separated themselves from the Black children and bunched together by the fireplace.

"C'mon, your mothers are waiting for you," Kenneth said, and he waved the four Webers out of the living room into the dining room and down the narrow hallway toward the kitchen.

The Weber children entered the kitchen with Kenneth and Barbara and Rita, Sam, and Delia coming along behind. The four rushed to Judith's and Claire's outstretched arms and embraced their mothers with tears of joy, as if the women had successfully negotiated with their captors for their release. In triumph Judith and Claire looked over the heads of their children at Kenneth and Barbara.

Kenneth said, "That performance . . . it only proves these kids are scared to death of you two," he said. "You might as well know, ladies, that as soon as you're gone, I'm calling Carol Evans at CPS."

The Weber family moved as a group to the door. Judith flashed a thin smile, her eyes cold and deadened. "You can call the fucking Gestapo if you want. No one's taking our children from us. No one."

Then they were gone, swallowed by the blowing snow and darkness.

Rita went into the playroom and switched on the television. "Who wants to watch *SpongeBob* with me?" She sounded almost relieved.

Sam and Delia joined their big sister in front of the screen.

Sam called out to the kitchen, "Daddy, they left their backpacks here."

Kenneth didn't respond. He was already dialing Carol Evans at CPS.

He had no way of anticipating what would follow. None of us did. We learned what happened to the Weber family only after the fact and gradually. Most of it had to be reconstructed from the accounts of only a few witnesses, starting with Barbara Odell, who saw the Webers early that morning with their four kids and two dogs in the maroon Ford SUV as it made its way down the driveway that Kenneth had plowed the previous afternoon. They turned right onto High Street, which had been cleared during the night by the Sam Dent town plows. Kenneth had left earlier for the prison in Lewis, and he himself did not see the Webers leave.

They were also spotted by the school bus driver, Dolores Driscoll, when she stopped to pick up the Odell kids by the mailbox. The sky was clear and sapphire blue, the blinding sunlight intensified by the snow. The Webers' SUV passed the Odell kids seconds ahead of the school bus. Rita, Sam, and Delia waved to the Webers, but no one in the vehicle acknowledged their presence. Dolores Driscoll picked up the Odell kids, and with them aboard, the school bus followed the Webers along High Street to where it joins Route 9. There the Webers' maroon SUV turned right, apparently leaving town, and the school bus turned left, headed for the Sam Dent Regional School.

The Webers stopped first at the North Country SPCA Animal Shelter in Westport, where they dropped off their two dogs. They said they were going on a long road trip and could no longer care for them and wanted to place them for adoption. The shelter, a no-kill shelter, gladly accepted the animals. They were healthy and placid and still young and would be easily and quickly adopted. It's a popular breed, American pit bull terriers.

The young woman who managed the shelter, Melody Schwartz, 28, later said that the woman who drove the SUV did not come in with the dogs or sign them over to the shelter. That was all done by the one named Claire Weber, who had a southern accent. She provided Schwartz with a file folder containing the dogs' medical and vaccination records, all up to date, and a book bag filled with what she said were the dogs' favorite toys and a barely used twenty-pound bag of organic dry dog food. Then Claire Weber left the shelter and got into the front passenger seat of the SUV, and the family drove away.

Melody Schwartz later stated that from the shelter office window she could see the two White women in front and the four Black children of various ages in back, and they all seemed calm and content, as if indeed they were embarking on an extended road trip. "They didn't come in and say goodbye to the dogs, like people usually do when they drop off their family pets," she said. "Most times it's really sad for a family when they have to give up their pet dog or cat for adoption. People cry sometimes. But these kids and the other lady, the driver, they all stayed in the car, and the kids seemed half asleep and not to care, and the two White ladies acted like they were in a hurry to get going. The way they acted, I wondered if the kids even knew that their dogs were being given up for adoption. Maybe they thought they were just being dropped off to be boarded. But it wasn't my business, and I didn't want to interfere," she said.

From the animal shelter, the Weber family traveled north on Route 9, passing through the town of Keeseville, where they were videotaped by security cameras at a Stewart's convenience store located at the corner of Main and Pleasant Streets. While Claire Weber was inside the store purchasing a box of forty-eight Benadryl gelcaps and a six-pack of Dr Pepper, the driver, Judith Weber, got out of the SUV and topped off the tank with $12.33 worth of gasoline. The gasoline and the Benadryl and Dr Pepper were all charged to Claire Weber's Visa card. In the video, the children in the back of the vehicle appear to be asleep. Blood tests and evidence at the Weber home later indicated that before they departed that morning the contents of four Benadryl gelcaps had been mixed into each child's oatmeal, the taste apparently disguised by a large addition of maple syrup or some other yet to be determined sweetener.

North of Keeseville, Route 9 winds along the western bank of the tumbling, rock-strewn Ausable River as it makes its way to Ausable Chasm. The narrow three-mile gorge squeezes the leisurely, north-flowing river into a torrent that roars through the chasm and on the other side suddenly broadens and slows and a few miles farther north empties into the vast waters of Lake Champlain. The sky remained clear, the day cold and bright in sunlight reflected off the snow, the road mostly plowed but still coated with a slippery, inch-deep, crusty slush. There was almost no traffic that morning. Every few miles a state or county or town plow rumbled past in one direction or the other, yellow roof lights flashing and salt spreader at the back spitting rock salt into the slush. No one was out this morning who did not have to be out.

A few miles short of the chasm, the SUV pulled into an Adirondack Park trailhead parking area with an open view of the river and remained parked for approximately forty-five minutes, where again the vehicle and its passengers were caught by a security camera. It is assumed, from the empty Dr Pepper soda cans and pink-and-blue Benadryl carton discovered the following day in the park trash container, that the children were administered a second dose of the antihistamine at this location.

From here on there were no witnesses to contribute to our understanding of what happened. At 11:05 a.m. an orange Clinton County plow truck driven by a man named Edgar Sneed, 42, resident of Plattsburgh, was spreading salt on Route 9 coming from the north. As he drove over Ausable Chasm, he noticed that a section of the chest-high steel guardrail on his right between the pedestrian walkway and the edge of the bridge had broken loose and was dangling in the air one hundred feet above the roaring water.

Sneed drove over the bridge to the Keeseville side and

pulled into the public parking lot. The park and public facil-
ities were empty, closed for the season. He set the brake
and left the engine running and the bar of yellow roof lights
flashing and stepped down from his truck and walked back
along the sidewalk to the break in the guardrail. The bolts
that had attached the flimsy fencing to the concrete walkway were sheared off. He looked over at the torrent below
and saw the undercarriage of a maroon Ford Explorer, and
his legs went wobbly, and he backed away from the opening
to a place where the railing was intact and he felt safe again.
He clung to the railing with both hands and looked down
at the river a second time, at the chassis and the wheels
and the black underbelly of the vehicle, at the doors blown
open by the explosive force of the crash. The car was fifteen
or twenty yards downstream from the bridge. It must have
been moving at high speed when it hit the guardrail and
went off the bridge and flipped over and smashed roof-first
into the icy river, crushing whoever was inside.

The water tumbled and swirled over and around the
boulders and sedimented sandstone slabs, gushing past
the SUV on both sides. Sneed saw several bodies half out
of the vehicle being dragged by the churning water farther into the river. They were White people's bodies and
Black. From this distance he couldn't tell anything more
about them than their race. He studied the tire tracks on
the bridge, those he hadn't erased with his truck. There
was no sign of a slide or swerve in the icy slush, no sign of
an accident or loss of control. Instead, the tracks jumped
the curb at an angle perpendicular to the road and crossed
the sidewalk to where they disappeared into open space. It

was as if, coming from the Keeseville side, the driver had stopped halfway over the gorge, then backed up to the curb, turned the SUV hard to the left and stomped on the gas pedal and driven straight through the guardrail and off the bridge into the air and down.

Sneed returned to his truck, where he'd left his cell-phone, and called 9-1-1. He said there was a bad accident on the bridge over Ausable Chasm and they should send an EMT unit at once. But it'll be tricky, he told the dispatcher, because the car went off the bridge into the river. "The car's upside down," he said in a trembling voice. "And the people inside it, they appear to be dead. They're at the bottom of the gorge just downstream from the Route 9 bridge," he said. "Maybe they're not all dead. I don't know. Maybe there are some survivors. But . . . but I can't reach them from here," Sneed said and almost started to weep. He caught himself and said that the park was locked down and closed for the season. He said he'd stay and block oncoming vehicles from crossing the bridge until the state cops showed up.

That should be the end of the story. But it isn't.

An autopsy on the bodies found in the SUV and in the river downstream from the vehicle provided no evidence of alcohol or drugs, except for the antihistamine in the bodies of the children, who were thought to be asleep when the car went off the bridge. An Essex County coroner's inquest was convened in Elizabethtown, the county seat, and after two days of testimony, the jurors ruled unanimously that Judith and Claire Weber were guilty of the premeditated murder of their four children and had died by suicide. Evidence gathered from the SUV's event data recorder, or black box, and the Weber women's cellphones and home computer—along with the testimony of Melody Schwartz, who ran the animal shelter, and Edgar Sneed, who described the tire tracks in the semifrozen slush on the bridge, which melted before anyone thought to photograph them—supported the coroner's report and confirmed Judith and Claire Weber's suicidal and murderous intentions. The cellphones of both women and the couple's home computer were found to have been used in Google searches for the effects of an overdose of Benadryl and death by hypothermia. The black box in the couple's Ford Explorer confirmed that the driver, who was assumed to be Judith Weber, drove the vehicle against the guardrail with the accelerator at full throttle without once applying the vehicle's brakes. A New York State police officer testified that the driver and the five passengers were not wearing seatbelts.

No one, of course, could understand what led Judith and Claire Weber to commit such a horrid act, not even Barbara and Kenneth Odell, who had lived next door to the Weber family and were thought to have known them better than anyone else in town. In the weeks after the crash the Odells repeatedly told their neighbors and acquaintances and the dozens of journalists and TV camera crews and reporters who descended on the town that the Webers had seemed like a decent couple, devoted, conscientious parents, a little odd, maybe, but not in any way that made them likely to have done such a terrible thing to their children, whom they seemed to love. Kenneth Odell was particularly emphatic about that. "No, those women loved their kids. They loved them the same as we love ours. That's why it's so hard to fathom."

The principal of the public school, Ellen Shipley, declined to comment on the Webers, except to say that, after the Weber women decided to homeschool their children, she had lost touch with them. In the aftermath of what she called "the incident," her main concern was whether to hire a grief counselor for the regularly enrolled Sam Dent schoolchildren. She claimed not to have known the Weber women very well personally.

The Odells couldn't explain to their own children, Rita, Sam, and Delia, what had happened. They couldn't explain it to each other or to themselves, either. They did not know why it had happened or how it could have been avoided. They believed that there was nothing that anyone in town or anyone working for the county or state social services might have done to save those four children from being murdered and their two mothers from committing suicide. Nothing.

Beneath those unanswered questions slumbered another. Had Kenneth and Barbara Odell themselves inadvertently done or said something that caused Judith and Claire Weber to drug their children on that winter morning and drive them off the bridge into the chasm? That bothered them the most. It was the question they least wanted to ask, the question they least wanted to answer.

Ultimately, Ellen Shipley decided not to hire a grief counselor. It wasn't as if the homeschooled Weber kids had been the Sam Dent public school kids' classmates. Nonetheless, Rita and Sam and Delia Odell heard stories, rumors, and gossip from the other kids at school and on Dolores Driscoll's bus. Children are intrepid purveyors of tales told about adults, especially tales that tell of cruelty, betrayal, and abandonment of children by their parents. The Odell kids naturally paired their home and family with the now-empty house next door and the family that had lived there, causing them to ask Kenneth and Barbara repeatedly if the Weber mothers really did kill their children and themselves on purpose like everyone at school was saying.

Kenneth and Barbara could not speak truthfully about what the Weber mothers had done and what they themselves had done and not done. So they lied. They said no, of course the Weber mothers didn't kill their children. It was an accident. A terrible accident. It was caused by the snow and by the icy condition of the road and bridge. It was tragic, but it was no one's fault.

Rita and Sam and even little Delia didn't believe them. Nobody else in town thought the death of the Webers was no one's fault. Why should they? The suicide of the parents and the murder of their four children was a crime, not an accident, right? And if a crime, it needed a criminal. And if there was a criminal, there had to be a motive. Kenneth and Barbara weren't about to give their children a criminal or a motive.

At a certain point they simply refused to discuss any further what happened to Judith and Claire Weber and their four kids. They refused to speak about it with their children or between themselves or with anyone in town. No more, that's the end of it.

In the spring Barbara decided to locate her vegetable garden, not out of sight on the far side the house, as she'd earlier planned, but in the meadow in front of the house, adjacent to the now-overgrown plot where the Weber family had cultivated their garden. By mid-June, to her delight and surprise, it was a great horticultural success, fully as bountiful as the Webers' garden had been. She learned to can and preserve pickles and beans and make jams, and her squashes and pumpkins and tomatoes won ribbons that fall at the Essex County Fair. From a goat farm in Vermont, Barbara and Kenneth brought home a pair of baby Alpine goats and named them Namby and Pamby, a female and a male, and assigned them to the kids, who were responsible for raising and eventually milking Namby twice a day and grooming and showing the pair at the fair alongside their mother's produce. The family rescued a mixed-breed dog named Hooter, part beagle and part golden retriever, from the North Country SPCA. At their parents' urging, the kids renamed him Scooter. They added a dozen chickens and a rooster for the eggs, but when Barbara and the kids pleaded for a donkey, Kenneth put his foot down—enough, no donkey.

Judith Weber's only living relative, a first cousin named Reed Weber, inherited the property. A retired pharmacist from Ohio, he'd never actually been inside the house, although he'd seen plenty of black-and-white photographs of the place from his and Judith's parents' and grandparents' time. The same realtor who had represented the Odells the year before listed it furnished for what the Odells had paid for theirs, $110,000. Three months later, when no one had made an offer on the property or attended the realtor's open-house showings, except for the few of us from town who'd gone out of curiosity, Reed Weber dropped the asking price by five percent, then three months later by another five.

It was unsettling to visit the house. Not that it felt haunted. Quite the opposite. It felt as if the married couple who had been living there was still in residence, still homeschooling their kids, and out of politeness had absented themselves while strangers wandered through the rooms and hallways and bathrooms and checked out the attic tower and the basement and the attached carriage barn. As we strolled from room to room, we averted our gaze from the previous inhabitants' clothing and boots and coats and hats and neatly made beds and did not peek into the bedroom closets or dresser drawers. We wore medical masks because of the Covid pandemic, which somehow made us feel even more invasive and detached. In the dining room, which appeared to have served as the children's classroom, and in the kitchen, crayoned drawings of animals and smiling mixed-race families at play beneath sunny skies were tacked to the walls and taped to the refrigerator door.

From time to time we stopped and looked out the tall windows at the duplicate house next door, where the Odells lived. Barbara and the three children, hoes and rakes in hand, and their dog, Scooter, stood in the vegetable garden on the far side of High Street, and Kenneth sat on his John

Deere mower in the middle of the wide sloped lawn. The Odells were looking back at us.

The realtor had placed on the kitchen table a stack of printed brochures describing the property in glowing terms and a legal pad where anyone interested in making an offer could write their name, phone number, and email address, and she'd get back immediately. We left the brochures untouched, and no one wrote their contact information on the yellow pad.

The absentee owner, Reed Weber, kept reducing the price, but the house remained unsold. Finally, Weber stopped paying the taxes and insurance on the place, and last April the town of Sam Dent seized the property, and the tax collector put it up for sale at auction. Kenneth and Barbara Odell were the only bidders, and the town had no choice but to accept their opening bid of $5,000, which barely covered the delinquent taxes and legal fees.

It's unclear what the Odells plan to do with the house and carriage barn. The land alone is worth more than what they paid for the property. Most of us in town say that, if it were ours, we'd hire a demolition company to bulldoze the buildings and haul the wreckage away and let grass grow over it.

★

KIDNAPPED

I TOOK MY AFTERNOON WALK with my dog. We climbed along the trail that winds uphill in a switchbacked, clockwise loop from our house in Sam Dent through the woods along a rumpled ridge and back down to the house. The understory is thick and brush impacted, the overstory leafy and low. There are no grand views up there of the surrounding mountains and valleys and the village. The woods itself is the scenery.

It's a forty-five-minute hike. The trail, mapped and marked and maintained by my wife and me over the decades that we have lived here, passes uphill through dense stands of birch and oak and maple and poplar, a tree the locals call popple. At the top and along the north-facing ridge, the mix of hardwoods is displaced by a descending grove of conifers, mostly scrub pine and balsam. Every spring my wife and I clear the trail of blowdown and rake away the previous autumn's mouldering leaves that would otherwise obscure the trail and encourage new growth, or our way through the woods would soon be lost to us. Sometimes we are forced to reroute the trail around the immovable fallen trunk of a mature tree uprooted by a winter gale. In spring the trail often erodes in places and turns to mud, and we shift it to higher, drier ground nearby. In these small ways the trail keeps changing, and the changes add up, until after a decade or so we no longer remember its original route.

I thought about that, and then I thought about how the lumber companies scalped the hills and valleys in the nineteenth and early twentieth centuries, before shifting south to clear-cut the forests of Georgia and the Carolinas. For a few generations, local farmers pastured cows and sheep and kept the land bald, save for a few scattered oak and chestnut trees nurtured to shade the grazing herds, until the farmers and herdsmen, too, abandoned these bare northern hills for flatter, greener pastures in the Midwest and West or for city and suburban life.

A few solitary, century-old oak and chestnut trees spared to shade the livestock remain, surrounded now by robust second- and third-growth trees. They are almost invisible, until you find yourself standing next to one. Our switchbacking trail passes near one ancient oak in the middle of a birch and popple grove on the way up and another located in among the scrub pines on the way down. They no longer produce descendants. Their bark is crumpled and withered. They are lightning struck and wind torn, split and scarred, and many of the largest branches are leafless and about to fall. Fungi—chicken-of-the-woods and mazegill and bracket—cling like carbuncles to their thickened, corrugated bark.

Were it not for these old oaks, isolatos among the younger hardwoods and conifers, we would think this was the same forest now as when it was threaded by paths made by the Iroquois and Algonquin natives crossing seasonally from the St. Lawrence valley to the Hudson, before the arrival of the white people with their steel axes and saws and their plows and domesticated animals. We would think it was the forest primeval itself, timeless, unchanging, the way the world at this exact crossing of longitude and latitude and altitude and soil and climate was meant to be and had always been.

But we would be wrong. A second-growth forest is not the same as a first, and a third is not the same as a second. Those old dying oak and chestnut trees saved a century ago from ax and saw to shade the grazing livestock are surrounded now by all the wrong progeny—birches and popple in one case, pine trees in the other. Absent a mature overstory's broad canopy, the understory receives too much unfiltered light, and low thickets and dense copses of trees and shrubs all the same age spring up.

In ancient times a carpet of fallen leaves and ferny ground cover was lit by long beams of sunlight descending from openings in the treetops as if from the clerestory windows of a great cathedral. Humans and other animals walked easily among the tall straight trunks and had unobstructed views from glen to vernal pond and stream to the glacial moraine beyond. That was a forest, not a woods. But the forest was not replaced by itself. It was displaced and replaced by these woods, which is a different and lesser thing.

My dog darted through the brush ahead of me, tracing the lingering spoor of a deer or bear or coyote, led by his nose instead of our man-made trail. And as I walked I remembered again a story from the village, part of which I saw, part of which I heard from witnesses, and part of which I imagined.

The story, as it shaped itself in my memory and imagination, began one night in August of 2019, a few months after Franklin and Elizabeth Dent, known locally as Frank and Bessie Dent, sold their house in town. They moved their twenty-year-old grandson, Steven, whom they called Stevie, into a single-wide trailer they bought for him on Route 9N and took up living in the one-story, one-bedroom, prefab log house they'd built on a wooded forty-acre lot up on Irish Hill that had been in Frank's family for generations.

Frank and Bessie had designed their house on Irish Hill several years earlier for their coming old age—all the rooms on one floor, door openings wide enough for a wheelchair though neither had need for one yet, kitchen cabinets low and easy to reach, walk-in shower and grab bars in the bathroom, ramps leading to the front and back doors, and an attached, heated garage for their Subaru Outback. They were rational pessimists, the kind of people who anticipate disaster and make careful plans to avoid it. Stevie didn't object to the move. He said he'd intended to find a place of his own anyhow. The single-wide on 9N a few miles from his grandparents' home suited him perfectly, he said.

That was the night Frank and Bessie were kidnapped. But the story doesn't begin there. It began years earlier. They had both retired at seventy—Frank from Gordon Oil Company in Ausable Forks, where for forty-two years he had worked his way up from driver to office manager, Bessie from the Lake Placid branch of Adirondack Bank and Trust, where she had been a teller. She started at the bank right out of high school and quit in 2005 in order to raise Stevie and returned eight years later when Stevie started high school.

Stevie's father, Chip, Frank and Bessie's only child, was killed by a roadside bomb in Iraq in 2004, leaving behind Chip's twenty-three-year-old widow and six-year-old son. The widow, Amy Dent (née Clarkson), from an old, respected Sam Dent family, got into drugs, or she was already into drugs and Chip didn't know about it or he never would have enlisted to go to Iraq to fight the terrorists. But after he was killed and his remains brought back and buried, she was arrested a few times and was in and out of rehab. Frank and Bessie took in Stevie, until finally we heard Amy had run off with her biker boyfriend for someplace down south, New Orleans or Miami, where after a few years she was rumored to have died of an overdose. In town it was kind of expected. Her parents, both of whom had dementia, were living by then in a retirement home in Plattsburgh where children weren't allowed, so Frank and Bessie raised Stevie as if he were their son, and they loved him dearly.

Because of their grief over having lost their son in the

Iraq War, they loved their grandson even more than they had loved Chip at the same age. Also, when they were raising Stevie they were older, if not wiser, in their late fifties and sixties, with most of their life behind them. Some people, as they grow old, live in the past, because there's more of it. Others live in the future, despite there being less of it. Frank and Bessie lived in the future.

For them, the past, after the loss of Chip, was tainted by grief and guilt. After the 9/11 attack on the World Trade Center, Chip, like most Americans, believed that it was his patriotic and religious duty to fight and defeat the Muslim terrorists. Frank encouraged him to enlist in the Marines, just as his father, a World War Two veteran, had urged Frank to join the Marines and go to Vietnam to fight and defeat the godless Communists. For different reasons than Frank's, Bessie also encouraged Chip to enlist. She was no friend of her son's marriage to Amy Clarkson and hoped the wartime separation might tempt Amy to leave him. Bessie had already begun back then to imagine raising Stevie herself with Frank until Chip found himself a new and more stable, drug-free wife. Chip was a good catch, handsome and athletic, with an associate's degree from Adirondack Community College, and he had his old job as a lineman for New York State Electric & Gas waiting for him when he returned from Iraq. Chip loved little Stevie, and Bessie believed that, if he had lived, Chip would have fought for custody in the divorce, and Amy, with her drug history, would have had to give him up.

After Chip was killed, Bessie preferred not to remember those thoughts and plans. Frank tried to forget telling Chip that, because of the radical Islamic attacks of September 11, 2001, if he was a young man, he'd be headed to Iraq alongside him. For different reasons, Bessie and Frank felt guilty for the way things had turned out. But forgetfulness was easier of access and less complicated than regret. So Frank and Bessie lived in the future, and for them the future was Stevie.

They doted on the child and bent their will and wishes to his and believed that he was brilliant and beautiful, and they rarely hesitated to say so. At Bessie's urging, they had become regular parishioners at the Westport Bible Church, even though it meant a seventeen-mile drive from their home and back. The too-liberal minister of the Congregational church in Sam Dent had married a gay couple, two women, and they'd had enough. They enjoyed telling the story of how, whenever they were in the parking lot of the Westport Bible Church, Stevie, who was only five then and in kindergarten, called out random-seeming numbers as they walked past the parked cars: "Seventy-seven!" "Ninety-one!" "Forty-three!" The way Frank told it, one Sunday morning, walking from their car to the church door, he followed the boy's gaze and realized that he was adding up and calling out the sums of the individual numbers on the license plates. Bessie credited Stevie's love of numbers to Pastor Rob Williston's habit of quoting chapter and verse from the Bible by number. Frank said it proved he was a little Einstein, a genius. It's possible they were both right.

Some folks in town, friends of Frank and Bessie, who were themselves no longer raising young children but remembered their own when they were Stevie's age and had grandkids whom they saw frequently, thought that actually Stevie was unexceptional and just spoiled. The kindergarten teacher, Elsa McCann, did not think he was a genius. She had taken a child psychology course at Plattsburgh State and believed Stevie had serious anger issues and might be borderline mentally ill. She didn't know in what way, exactly. The other children were a little afraid of him, and she could hardly wait until he moved on to first grade. He seemed to have no friends but appeared not to care, as long as he had his grandparents' love and constant attention. He rarely spoke to others, whether children or adults, but when at home he talked constantly to Frank and Bessie, telling them in a jumble of words in frequently disconnected sentences everything that passed through his mind, which they took to be a further sign of his genius.

Bessie sometimes worried about Stevie's strange behavior and lack of friends, but Frank said, "Really smart kids like Stevie, they play the game by different rules than the rest of us." The boy did not seem unhappy or lonely, Frank pointed out. He enjoyed showing off to his grandparents, who understood him and loved him without restraint and raised him restriction-free. "He withholds himself from the other kids on purpose," Frank said. "Kids with normal IQs and interests, they probably bore him. Chip was a little like that when he was a kid," he reminded her.

Despite Frank's reassurance, Bessie was afraid that Stevie's mother's genes and her drug addiction and Chip's departure for Iraq and subsequent disappearance from Stevie's life, even though he was little more than a toddler when all this happened, had combined to warp Stevie's young psyche in ways that did not necessarily produce signs of genius. It occurred to her from time to time that their grandson was "mentally disturbed"—Bessie would not say "mentally ill"—and as he grew older and exhibited increasingly odd and antisocial behavior, first in elementary school and later in middle and high school, she watched him with growing fear.

She wasn't afraid of him; he was extremely passive and nonviolent. She was afraid *for* him. In Sam Dent, except for the few who are homeschooled, all the children from kindergarten through twelfth grade attend the same school. There are usually thirteen to fifteen students to a class, and they are classmates from early childhood to early adulthood and grow up almost like first and second cousins. It's tribal, practically familial, and the roles they acquire early they keep all the way to graduation and beyond, when they become adult members of the community. Except for the few who move away for college or the military or marry someone from another part of the country, they retain the roles they acquired as children all the way to old age and decrepitude, and after they're gone that's how people remember them.

From the start, little Stevie Dent was the self-selected outsider, the deliberate loner, the boy and eventually the man who, except in the company of his grandparents, kept his thoughts, opinions, and feelings to himself. And he was indeed little, slightly built and always the shortest member of his class, even shorter than the girls and later the women, topping out when he was eighteen at five feet four inches. In that sense, as Bessie feared, Amy's genes were kicking in, for she had been a tiny woman, barely five feet in height and weighing less than ninety pounds. Stevie's dad, Chip, like Frank and Bessie, had been tall and muscular and well proportioned and athletic. Chip had been a varsity-level athlete in three sports all through high school and after graduation played first base for the Beavers town team alongside his dad. Frank for many years was the catcher for the Sam Dent Beavers, the men's town softball team, and Bessie was an avid ice skater and cross-country skier. Stevie, though, never tried out for any team and was not known to have participated even in nonteam sports, like golf or fly-fishing or hunting. Which is unusual in a town like Sam Dent, where athletics, sports, are a way of life, a maker and marker of social status and value.

After high school, Stevie turned his part-time summer job at the Willow Wood Nursery into a full-time year-round position and continued living in town with his grandparents, who had not yet moved into their small, carefully planned retirement house on Irish Hill. He no longer attended church with Frank and Bessie, which saddened them, especially Bessie. Frank assured her that Stevie would eventually find Jesus on his own, just as they had. For graduation—at the bottom of a class of fourteen—Frank gave his grandson a new shark-gray Ford F-150 pickup, although he financed and registered it in his own name. Stevie enjoyed driving the truck and never walked anywhere if he could drive it, and he liked working at the nursery. The long, silent, solitary hours spent outdoors all summer transplanting and weeding and composting and watering the flowers and shrubs and seedlings and saplings calmed him, and in winter he was glad for the humidity and fan-blown heat of the greenhouse and loved the turbid odor of the black soil in the beds.

Because of Stevie's evident lack of ambition and his uncomplaining, solitary ways, the couple who owned and managed the nursery, Benny and Cecilia Brown, thought he was perfect for the job. "Stevie's been a steady worker from Day One, reliable and honest and on time," Benny said to the reporter for the *Adirondack Weekly Harbinger* who came to the nursery to question the Browns about Stevie after the news broke that his mother had been killed and his grandparents kidnapped.

"He doesn't talk much under the best of circumstances. Don't be surprised if he won't talk to you, especially now," Benny told the reporter. He was correct. Stevie did not agree to be interviewed, not then, not later. Not ever.

The kidnapping occurred on the night of August 16 in 2019, where I began this story. It was after supper, the dishes were washed and dried and put away, and Frank and Bessie were trying to watch *America's Got Talent* on their new flat-screen TV, but Frank kept screwing up the remote commands and couldn't find the channel. Finally he passed the remote over to Bessie.

"You do it, you're so darn smart," he said and got up from his La-Z-Boy recliner and walked to the deck window and looked out. There was still enough dusky light for him to see across the driveway to the road. "Times like this," he said, "we need Stevie," when a gray Ford F-150 with tinted windshield and side windows turned off the road into the driveway. "Well, whaddaya know? Seek and ye shall find," he said. "Knock and it shall be opened to you."

"That's Matthew, dear. Seven seven. Who is it?"

"Stevie."

"It's kind of late for him to drop by without calling. Nothing's wrong, I hope," she said.

"Probably needs a tool or a ladder or something. That trailer of his is pretty bare-bones," Frank said. He grabbed his red MAGA cap off the hook by the door and put it on and walked out to the deck and threw a grandfatherly wave of the hand at the truck as it pulled up and stopped, facing the garage. That's when Frank saw on the rear bumper the blue-and-white Quebec number plate with the motto that always annoyed him, because he didn't know what it meant—*Je me souviens*.

"It's not Stevie," he said. "It's Canadians. Canucks. Must be lost or something."

"The show's on, Frank! I got it!"

No one had stepped from the truck yet, and Frank couldn't see who was inside or how many there were. It was a SuperCrew with four doors and a rear bench seat, a year or two older than Stevie's F-150. He walked to the edge of the deck and stood at the top of the ramp, so the driver and passengers, if there were any, could see him. He waited for someone to get out or lower the window and ask for directions. Tourists, he figured. It was a Friday, and he wondered if it was a Canadian holiday weekend, their Thanksgiving or Independence Day or something. They should sync their national holidays with ours, he thought. It would make it easier for everyone.

The driver's and the front passenger's doors opened simultaneously, and two men emerged from the truck. One, the driver, was tall and gaunt, the other short and wide and bulging with muscles like a body builder, both wearing orange safety vests over bright yellow road-crew T-shirts with *SINTRA* printed across the front. For a second, Frank thought they were workers and must have crossed the border after work to drink at one of the north country roadhouses and took a wrong turn heading back to Canada. Something like that. Drunk, probably.

They got closer, and Frank saw that their heads were wrapped in women's nylon stockings knotted at the top. He removed his glasses and let them hang from his neck by the string and rubbed his eyes. The men looked like Martians. Then he realized that they were aiming handguns at him.

The taller one said, "Just stand there, *Papé*. Hands on the banister, and you will do okay." He spoke English with a diluted French accent. Red, blue, and green tattoos of serpents and saints crawled up his skinny arms and disappeared under the sleeves of his tee, reappearing at the neck.

"Yeah," the other said. "*Papé*."

Bessie called from the living room, "Frank, the show's on! You're going to miss it!"

"Is there anybody more here, *Papé*? Just you and the old lady?"

Frank shook his head no. His mouth was too dry to speak. His legs were trembling, and he clung to the railing, not because he'd been ordered to at gunpoint, but so he wouldn't fall.

"*Recueillir la grand-mère*," the man with the tattoos said to the other.

"No!" Frank cried. Without understanding French, he knew what the man meant. *La grand-mère* was Bessie.

"Don't worry. As long as you do what we say, nobody gonna get hurt."

"Yeah," said Muscles. He walked past Frank through the open door into the living room, and Frank heard Bessie scream. He heard Muscles say, "Shut the fuck up, *Mamie*."

Frank found his voice and called to her, "It's okay, just . . . just do what he says! Give them whatever they want!" He turned to Tattoos. "What *do* you want?" Frank thought he could detect a smile and a thatched mustache behind the mesh of the stocking mask.

"What have you got?"

"Nothing! We don't have any valuables," he said. "We don't keep any cash, except for groceries and such." He was talking fast now. "Credit cards? Want our credit cards? I'll give you our Adirondack Trust ATM cards, too, and the number codes, the PIN numbers. You can withdraw up to five hundred dollars with each card," he said. "Same with the credit cards. That's two thousand dollars in cash right there."

"Okay, okay. We'll tap the cards and the ATMs when we leave town. First we want you and *Mamie* in there to make a phone call for us." He waved his gun in the direction of the door. "Inside, *Papé*."

Frank let go of the railing and walked into the living room, and the tattooed gunman followed close behind.

Bessie, wide-eyed and blinking, looked up at Frank from the sofa expectantly, as if he could explain what was happening. She said, "Frank?"

Muscles stood behind her, gun at his side, watching *America's Got Talent* on the TV.

"They want our credit cards and ATM cards," Frank said. "And they want us to make a phone call."

"A phone call? To who?"

Muscles said, *"Avez-vous vu ce spectacle, Denis? C'est étrange."*

"Pas de nom, asshole," Tattoos snapped. "And stop watching the fucking TV," he said in English.

"Désolé."

Frank caught their meaning, if not the exact words. He wondered why the man didn't want them to know his name, his *nom*, when his tattoos identified him so well. The name was French anyhow, weird sounding, like a woman's. *Denee.* Frank couldn't have spelled it and knew he'd forget it. Not the tattoos, though. Or the muscles. He decided that the men were too stupid to be dangerous. He suddenly wasn't afraid of them. He hadn't been afraid of anyone since 1972, when he came back from Vietnam. If they were Americans, he knew that he and Bessie would be dead by now. These guys are clowns, he thought, French Canadians with guns. He decided to be nice to them.

Frank said, "Don't you have a phone of your own?"

"We need to use yours."

Frank said. "Those T-shirts and road crew vests. You guys really work for something called Sintra?"

"Why?"

"I dunno. Just curious."

Muscles said, "We used to work for them."

Denis said, "Shut the fuck up, Paul!"

"*Pas de nom, asshole,*" Paul said and laughed.

So it's Denee and Pole, Frank thought. Tattoos and muscles. Got it. In his mind he was already testifying at their trial. He said to Bessie, "Just be calm and do whatever they say. We'll be okay, I promise."

Denis asked if they had any guns in the house, and Frank said no.

Denis said, "Don't fucking lie to me, man. I know you got guns. You're American. Look at that hat you got on. You're a goddamn Donald Trump supporter. I'm not stupid. You got guns?"

Frank shrugged and led the men with Bessie back to the dressing room off his and Bessie's bedroom where he kept the metal gun cabinet. He liked showing off his firearms and rarely had the opportunity. He unlocked the cabinet with one of the dozen keys dangling from the carabiner that he wore clipped to his belt loop. Bessie said it made him look like a janitor, but he didn't care. He swung the door open. The cabinet held his M-16 and his .30-06 and his 20-gauge shotgun and his .22 caliber rifle and the two handguns, the Glock and the 9mm Springfield. There were a half dozen boxes of ammo on the shelf at the bottom of the cabinet.

"Sweet," Denis said.

Paul said, "How come you got so many fucking guns?"

"It's not so many. Well, for hunting," Frank said. "And in case of a home invasion, I guess."

Denis laughed. "What the fuck you think this is?" In

French he told Paul to put the guns and ammo in the truck under the false bed liner and walked Frank and Bessie back to the living room.

Frank sat on the sofa next to Bessie and pulled his cellphone from his pants pocket. He held it out and said, "Okay, so who do you want us to call? Or do you just want to borrow my phone?"

"Call your grandson."

"You mean Stevie?"

"Yeah, Steve. Stevie. Whatever. If he sees it's you, he'll pick up. He don't seem willing to answer when it's us. We spent all morning at his trailer and the afternoon at that place where he works, waiting for him to show up, but the guy has flied the coop."

"Why do you need to talk to Stevie?" Frank said.

"Don't worry about that. Just call him. When he answers, tell him hello so he knows it's you, and give me the phone," Denis said. "Switch it to speaker first," he added.

Frank nodded and put his glasses on. Bessie clutched his arm while he put the phone on speaker and punched in Stevie's number.

After the third ring, Stevie answered. "Hey, Pops, wussup?"

Frank said, "Stevie, there's someone here wants . . ."

Denis grabbed the phone, cutting him off. "I got your fucking grandparents here, Steve! You want to see them alive again, you know what you gotta do." A few seconds of silence passed. "Steve? I know you're listening. This is Denis, Steve," he said, and the phone went dead.

"Asshole!" Denis threw the phone down on the coffee

table. "I like you, *Papé*, but your grandson, he is a fucking asshole!"

Bessie scowled and said, "Don't you dare talk about Stevie that way! Shame on you!"

Paul entered the room. He spoke a few sentences in French that sounded like questions, and Denis answered, and Paul shook his head and bit his lower lip and looked disgusted.

Frank picked up his phone and turned to Denis. "You told Stevie, 'You know what you gotta do.' What do you mean by that? What's he gotta do? Maybe Bessie and me, maybe we can do it for him."

Denis said, "Your boy Steve, he has kept something that don't belong to him for longer than we agreed. Other than that, you don't need to know."

For a few minutes Denis quizzed Frank and Bessie about their grandson. He wanted to know where Stevie hung out when he wasn't at his trailer or working at the plant nursery.

They answered truthfully. He hung out with them, usually here, at their house, watching TV.

Denis asked for the names of his friends.

They said he didn't have any close friends, just acquaintances, people he'd gone to school with.

"No girlfriends?"

"No girlfriends."

"What about his mother, Amy? She have any friends here?"

Bessie said, "We don't have anything to do with her. And neither does Stevie."

Frank said, "We heard she was back in the area. But she's not tried to get in touch with him."

"She better not," Bessie said.

"Stevie would've told us if she had," Frank said.

Denis said their grandson Steve and his mom had business dealings with a few local people who did business with other local people. Denis and Paul were wholesalers, Steve and his mother did mainly retail. They dealt in and around Sam Dent, and their customers bought and sometimes resold. Denis wanted to know the names of the people Steve and his mother did business with.

But Stevie? Maybe Denis had him confused with someone else from town. Frank and Bessie knew there were several groups in and around Sam Dent, mostly young people, who bought and sold drugs—opioids, marijuana, meth, even heroin—and sometimes they gathered at drug-fueled parties after the Spread Eagle closed at eleven. A half dozen deaths and near deaths from overdosing in the region had recently made it to the evening news. Pastor Rob had given a series of blistering sermons on the topic last month at the Westport Bible Church. Frank and Bessie knew about drugs.

Stevie's mother, their daughter-in-law, had been a drug user. But that was fifteen or sixteen years ago, and she had abandoned him and left town and for years was rumored to have died somewhere down south of an overdose, and Stevie knew all about that, because Frank and Bessie had wanted him to know. They had raised Stevie to be as wary of drugs and his mother as they were. They'd heard she was alive and had come back to the north country and was living in Plattsburgh, but hadn't mentioned it to Stevie. Besides, Stevie was a loner, he never went to parties or hung out drinking at the Spread Eagle, and he had a steady job at the Willow Wood plant nursery and no loan on his truck to pay off or rent for his single-wide, thanks to the generosity of his grandparents, so he didn't need the money. Why would he sell drugs? Why would he be involved with his mother? Why would he be doing business with men like these two Canadians? There must be some terrible mistake. None of it made sense.

"You're looking for the wrong Steve Dent," Frank declared. "Steve's a pretty common name around here." But he was starting to think that maybe it did make sense. It was only a glimmer of an insight into his grandson's personality and character, and it contradicted everything that he had believed and said about him since the day they first took him into their home and raised him as their own. He thought about Stevie being abandoned by his mother and, in a deeply felt sense, by his father, too, and spending his childhood and adolescence in the care of two overprotective elderly people and always being the smallest kid in his class and possibly, despite what his grandparents claimed, not a genius, not even the brightest or cleverest kid in his class, and maybe he was, like his kindergarten teacher once said, mentally ill and not just different than normal kids. Okay, he was definitely different. But maybe that didn't mean what Frank and Bessie had taken it to mean.

These thoughts came to him as a jumbled, unsorted cluster of insights, and they filled him with sorrow and pity for his grandson, and for a moment he could imagine how the boy might have tried to make himself important and essential to the crowd, all the other young people in town who had never respected or especially liked him, by procuring drugs for them and their friends and the drug-using summer people from downstate. He could imagine Stevie selling the drugs too cheaply or maybe even giving them away to curry favor with them and not making enough money to pay back what he owed these Canadian dealers. He remembered the bartender at the Spread Eagle greeting Stevie as "Candyman" once when he and Bessie and Stevie went there for supper to celebrate his twentieth birthday.

He saw that his pride and vanity and his refusal to acknowledge the logic of her apprehensions had hurt both his wife and their grandson, and now it had placed his wife and grandson and him, too, in grave danger. And for a second he understood how his pride and vanity had contributed to the death in Iraq of his beloved son. Frank had pretended that Iraq was Vietnam. He had let himself think that he was his father and Chip was him. He had been wrong on all counts. He wanted to share these feelings and thoughts with Bessie. But he couldn't say them aloud to her in front of these men. He could barely say them in silence to himself.

Denis ordered Frank and Bessie to pack a suitcase. "Just what you need for a short vacation. Also a sweater or a jacket. Where we're going, man, it's colder than here."

"Where are we going?" Bessie asked.

Denis laughed. "Canada."

Paul asked in French why they couldn't just wait around for Steve to show up. Denis said because of the kid's mother. Don't forget her, the fucking bitch. They can't let the old couple loose. If Steve wants to see his grandparents again, he'll have to come up to Canada and bring what he owes them.

Frank caught the gist and said, "I think I get it. What do you want from Stevie? How much does he owe you? Maybe you'd take a personal check?"

Denis switched to English. "If Steve gets busted with what he owes us, the cops and the newspapers, they'll say it's one point five million dollars on the street or something. Okay? Or two million. Or three. The truth is all he owes us is three hundred fifty thousand American dollars in cash or unsold merchandise or a combination of the two. You got that much in your checking account, *Papé*?"

Frank said, "My God!"

Denis pulled off his stocking mask, and Paul did the same. "We don't need these now," Denis said.

They weren't bad-looking men. Both were in their forties and looked like what their T-shirts said they were, construction workers employed by Sintra. Paul was round-faced and had a gristly beard the same length as the buzz-cut hair on his scalp. Denis had narrow, scrutinizing eyes and a chestnut-colored thatch of a mustache and blue-streaked hair that matched his tattoos and a long shank of a ponytail. He pulled a crumpled half-empty pack of Gauloises from his vest side-pocket and lit a cigarette and inhaled deeply and sighed. "*Allons-y, mes amis*," he said. "Let's move."

Denis and Paul marched the couple at gunpoint back to the dressing room off Bessie's and Frank's bedroom, where Frank pulled a suitcase down from an overhead closet shelf and the two hurriedly packed it with a few days' clothing.

Bessie said, "Don't forget our pills and meds, Frank," and he went into the bathroom and scooped up their drugs—atenolol for his hypertension, allopurinol for his gout flare-ups, Xeljanz for her rheumatoid arthritis, Nexium for his heartburn, and Miralax for her constipation—and placed them in the suitcase.

"What about our passports?" Frank asked. "For crossing the border to Canada, I mean."

"They're in the desk in the living room," Bessie said.

Denis laughed. "The route we're taking, you won't need them," he said. "But it's a good idea. Me and Paul can always use a couple American passports. And wear that Trump hat," he said to Frank. "In case we run into a nosy local or a state cop."

Frank and Bessie collected their passports and handed them over to Denis, along with their credit and ATM cards and the cash from their wallets—less than one hundred dollars between them, grocery money. Denis held out his palm for their driver's licenses, too. "New York driver's licenses, they might come in handy someday," he said.

Frank felt oddly naked. He squared his red MAGA cap on his head and felt better.

They put Bessie in the back seat of their pickup with Paul beside her, his pistol in his lap, and Frank in front in the passenger seat. Denis drove. They stopped first at the Stewart's in the village, and Denis stepped out to gas up the truck. It was a little after nine, and the gray F-150 with

Quebec plates was the only vehicle in the lot. A curtain of darkness surrounded the harshly lit gas pumps and parking area. In the distance they could make out the dim window lights of the Spread Eagle Tavern and the outlines of a dozen parked cars. The rest of the village was shrouded in darkness.

Denis said, "This fucking town goes to bed early."

While he pumped the gas with one hand, Denis pulled a sheet of paper toweling from the dispenser with the other and passed it through the window to Frank and told him to write down the PIN numbers for their accounts.

Frank and Bessie used the same four-digit code for all their cards, and he wrote the numbers with his Gordon Oil Company ballpoint pen slowly, as if having trouble remembering them. He thought of making a run for it, but he couldn't leave Bessie alone in the truck with Paul and his pistol. He glanced around the lot and into the store, searching for someone he knew, a friend, a neighbor, a person he could somehow signal that he and Bessie were being kidnapped. Maybe he could tip him off with a wink and a nod, and the friend or neighbor would call the state police base in Ray Brook, and the troopers would race to their rescue.

The lot was empty, and there were no customers in the store. Just the daydreaming, nose-ringed high-school kid in his Stewart's maroon visor cap behind the counter and the white-haired fellow in his late seventies who Frank knew as Ralph from Upper Jay, who'd recently been let go from his day job as a greeter at Walmart and now, despite his age, had to work nights at Stewart's to make his rent money. "Poor planning," Frank had said to Bessie when describing the man to her. "Bad decisions. Nobody's fault but his own."

Denis topped off the tank and retrieved from Frank the paper towel with the PIN numbers and strolled into the mini-mart, where he ran their ATM cards and credit cards for as much cash as the machine would cough up, one thousand American dollars, all in twenties. He paid Ralph from Upper Jay with cash for the gas and a six-pack of Budweiser Lite and two large bags of Cheetos. He folded the wad of bills in half and shoved it like a thick sandwich into the side pocket of his orange vest and returned to the truck.

He didn't think about the fingerprints he'd left on the numerical keypad of the ATM machine, although he probably should have. He could have used the paper towel with Frank's telltale handwriting to wipe the keypad clean before he crumpled and tossed it into the trash container next to the gas pump. But he didn't, and at 11:30 that night, when Ralph from Upper Jay locked the door and switched off the fluorescent lights above the gas pumps, the balled-up piece of paper towel was still lying on top of the trash. The next afternoon when he came to work the nose-ringed kid bagged the trash and dropped the bag into the dumpster behind the store, where it would lie for two more days and nights, until the state investigator in charge of the case wiped the ATM machine for fingerprints and thought to go through the dumpster at the Stewart's where the Canadian kidnappers had stopped for gas and cash and beer and Cheetos.

They drove north on Route 9N, a winding, dark, two-lane country road, and picked up the interstate highway,

Route 87, at Keeseville and went on to Plattsburgh, where the local cops were busy chasing down drunken and stoned students at Plattsburgh State and weren't likely to bother stopping a gray pickup truck with Quebec plates and an elderly couple and a pair of men who looked like off-duty construction workers, four Canadian day-trippers come down to shop at Walmart or Costco or BJ's. Denis kept to the speed limit and stayed safely behind the few cars in front of them and politely dimmed the headlights whenever a vehicle approached from the other direction. North of Plattsburgh they left the interstate at the Champlain exit and drove along a secondary road to the western shore of Lake Champlain and entered the village of Rouses Point, a few miles south of the Canadian border. It was very dark now, no cars passing them either way, nothing open for business, all the inhabitants asleep or trying to sleep.

In downtown Rouses Point, Denis turned left onto Pratt Street, then right onto Church Street, out of the village into the countryside, headed north again toward the border, where the narrow road hooked abruptly to the left and ran a few yards south of the border and parallel to it. He pulled the truck over to the right onto the gravel shoulder and stopped and kept the engine running. They were at the edge of a wide field ringed by brush and batches of willow and sumac. Paul stepped out and holding his gun on Frank and Bessie ordered them out. "We gonna take us for a little walk in the country," he said.

Bessie said, "Frank? Is he going to kill us, Frank?" Her voice was shaky, an old lady's voice. Frank had never heard her sound like that before.

He got out of the truck and took her hand in his and helped her slide over to the open door and down to the ground. "No. They need us alive. At least until Stevie gives them what they want from him."

Denis told Frank and Bessie to take their suitcase from the truck bed. He spoke several quick sentences in French to Paul and drove off, heading west along the American side of the border. Bessie and Frank stood in darkness next to their suitcase at the side of the road. Paul held his gun in one hand and a flashlight in the other, which he switched on, and walking beside the couple, he showed them a way from the road through the brush into the meadow beyond. He said, "All kinda Chinese and Mexicans cross here. The Mohawks and the Micmacs, they got a regular migrant express running. You fucking Americans, you all worried about Mexico and building Trump's wall, and meanwhile anybody who wants can walk across from Canada."

The high grass was wet with dew and slapped their legs. The suitcase started to feel heavy to Frank, and the ground was uneven, and he struggled and was relieved when they were out of the field and walking along a narrow unpaved road again. He felt suddenly old, the way Bessie had sounded earlier. He wondered if she felt the way she sounded, a confused, frightened old lady. He couldn't tell if he himself was confused or just scared. Or both. He was almost always solely one or the other and wasn't used to feeling the two.

Gradually they made out the shape of a dairy barn and a two-story brick house in the near distance. They knew they were in Canada now. They passed the darkened farm, and a hundred yards beyond the house and barn they stepped off the road onto a cutout. Paul told them to move into the brush out of sight and set the suitcase down and rest. Frank gestured for Bessie to sit on the suitcase, and he stood beside her, as if posted to protect her.

Paul's tone had changed. He told them not to worry, Denis would pick them up soon. He spoke kindly to them, now that they were in Canada. He slipped his pistol into his vest side-pocket and asked if they were hungry, and Frank said no, but Bessie said yes, and Paul said that when Denis came for them they could have some Cheetos and split a beer. "He won't take long. He knows them customs guys at the border. Both sides, the Canadians and the Americans."

Frank said, "How far is it from here to where we're going?"

"Maybe an hour and a half," Paul said. He switched off the flashlight, and they were surrounded by darkness. Back at the farm a dog woke and barked twice, then gave it up. Frank looked at the lapis sky and the vast swirls of the galaxy embedded like bits of pyrite in the dark blue dome. It was the same cold, hard sky he saw on clear nights at home when he walked in the front yard after Bessie had gone to bed and he was still restless and unable to sleep and was deciding whether to pour himself a glass of Scotch whisky. But the Canadian sky seemed different than the American sky that hovered above his and Bessie's new log home on Irish Hill in Sam Dent, the four-square post-and-beam house they'd built and fitted out specifically for their retirement years. It was as if he was looking up from a different planet than friendly old planet Earth. He wished he could pour himself a glass of whisky now. He had not planned for anything that was happening tonight. He thought that he had planned for everything. Obviously he hadn't.

Paul strolled a few yards down the road and stood with his back to them, legs spread, and peed into the roadside brush. Frank drew his cellphone from his pocket. Should he call Stevie, or just punch in 9-1-1? He remembered that he was no longer in the United States and hadn't okayed Verizon's international calling option. He couldn't call for help, and without cellular service, the GPS on his phone didn't know where he and Bessie had gone. Where were they? Where was Stevie, his only grandson, his only living blood relative? Was this how his and Bessie's family, the Dents, emblematic, legendary, the oldest name in the region, came to an end?

Starting when the boy was in kindergarten, Frank Dent often praised his grandson, Stevie, for being a direct descendant—through Frank himself and the boy's war-hero father, Chip, and distantly on Stevie's mother Amy's side—of Samuel (Sam) Dent, the man for whom our town was named. Sam Dent, the man, was the first permanent white resident of the valley, our town's founding father, and by making sure the town was named for himself, he'd become a legendary figure forever after. Dentville was not acceptable to him, nor was Denton nor simply Dent. A man with an Olympian ego, he had insisted that it had to be the one and only Sam Dent.

He was a Revolutionary War veteran originally from New Hampshire, a mapmaker, surveyor, hunting guide, eventually a real estate mogul and developer, as the wilderness settlement evolved from Indian land to white men's hunting and trapping preserve to logging camp to Revolutionary War veterans' farm village and part-time summer resort to what it is now, a hometown for eleven hundred disparate souls. Frank Dent was proud of his ancestral connection to Sam Dent and wanted Stevie to claim it for himself, but Stevie had showed little interest in making the claim.

An amateur genealogist, Frank had researched and constructed over the years a detailed family tree, and as soon as Stevie was able to read, Frank had spread a half dozen taped sheets of typing paper out on the kitchen table and traced the tree from its topmost branch, where he'd written Stevie's name and birthdate, down the thickening branches through seven generations of fathers and mothers, of grandfathers and grandmothers, of great-grandfathers and great-grandmothers, all the way to Samuel Dent, the taproot, born in 1751 in Keene, New Hampshire, and died in 1847 in the newly incorporated Essex County town of Sam Dent, New York.

In the 1780s, following the War of Independence, the impoverished federal government paid off its wage debt to land-poor veterans from northern New England with millions of newly seized wilderness acres in upstate New York that for millennia had belonged communally to the native peoples. Veterans of the war, second- and third-born farmers' sons from New Hampshire, Vermont, and Maine, left their parents' shrinking, subdivided lands to their older siblings and picked up their axes and hoes and wives and children and livestock and made their way into the vast, dark, barely arable forests where game was plentiful and timber abundant and there were rivers and lakes for floating the pelts and lumber and cold-climate crops like potatoes and turnips and beets south to Lake Champlain and Lake George on to the mighty Hudson all the way to the markets of Manhattan. As if the immense tracts of rivers and lakes and rolling hills and high mountain peaks were their birthright, the Yankee invaders mapped and surveyed and claimed and sold and resold the whole of it for themselves and their progeny.

A few of these first arriving white men were literate and ruthless and brought with them legal, financial, and political skills, which allowed them to acquire more than their fair share of the millions of acres of federally appropriated Indian land. Samuel Dent was one of these men. He began with his veteran's claim against the new government's plunder, forty hillside acres on the Ausable River plain between the mountains, but soon had acquired ten more, then twenty times as much, until he owned nearly two thousand acres between Lake Champlain and the Ausable River, a huge swath of forest and river valley, all the arable land that later became the town of Sam Dent.

When the freezing winds and six-month-long winter snows defeated most of his neighbors and sent them west to gentler climes and richer soil in Ohio and Indiana, he bought failed farmsteads for pennies an acre. He forged the signatures of dead veterans and made applications for land grants in their names, then signed the grants over to himself as if he'd legally purchased them. He surveyed unclaimed land and registered hundreds of acres in his own name at the county seat and evicted the families who had built their cabins there and out of ignorance or illiteracy or sloth had neglected to make the trek to the courthouse in Elizabethtown to file their deeds. In the 1820s he built a lakeside lodge for downstate urban sportsmen and made himself their hunting and fishing and mountain climbing guide and garrulous, tale-telling fireside host, and soon they returned with their friends from the city for more of the true American wilderness experience that was fast disappearing in the eastern states. He grew a long beard and wore buckskin clothing and a coonskin cap and cultivated an accent that reminded his downstate clients of James Fenimore Cooper's character Natty Bumppo. His lodgers from Manhattan sometimes called him Hawkeye and Deerslayer.

Sam Dent outlived all but one of his five children and his wife, Amelia, who was rumored to have been half Mohawk, fathered by a French Canadian Jesuit priest. In his 1847 last will and testament, he left the lakeside lodge and the original forty acres, which included Frank and Bessie's land on Irish Hill, to his surviving son, Harley, and deeded over the remaining 1,857 acres, most of it on both sides of the meandering Ausable River, to Essex County, on condition that the land be incorporated as the town of Sam Dent, that it be subdivided into ten-acre lots and sold at market rates to anyone who wished to be a citizen of the town, the proceeds to go to the maintenance of roads and other public services until such time as sufficient taxes could be gathered from the citizenry to pay for said costs and upkeep. The Essex

County commissioners happily complied and made and named the town Sam Dent, as its benefactor wished.

This then was Stevie Dent's lineage, his ancestral origin, his roots. Frank was too modest a man to say it outright, but he believed that it was his greatest gift to his grandson. Though tainted by its origins—wartime plunder and misappropriation and forgery and outright theft, self-aggrandizement and egoism and greed—the family connection to the man named Sam Dent was for Frank a point of great personal pride. He himself had not profited from the crimes and voracious temperament of his ancestor, except for inheriting the acreage on Irish Hill, where his and Bessie's retirement home now stood. Thus, like most of our fellow citizens, he was free to ignore his ancestor's ancient crimes and personal flaws and concentrate instead on the myth of a Christian white man from New England with an ax and a rifle carving an American village out of a howling, uninhabited wilderness.

Stevie, however, couldn't have cared less about his genetic connection to our town's founding father—until he did. It happened all of a sudden. Perhaps he was, as his kindergarten teacher suggested so long ago, "mentally ill," because, in spite of his not having demonstrated any intellectual or academic ability worthy of note, he was very fond of numbers. They were to him physical objects that he could line up like dominoes and arrange and rearrange in patterns that fascinated him. He was like a human calculator. As a child he could count cards and easily beat adults at poker and bridge and pinochle. To the adults' relief, he had little interest in card games, mainly because he had little interest in other people, and games brought him into contact with other people.

His interest in his grandfather's family tree came about one night three months and a week before his grandparents were kidnapped. He was sitting alone in the single-wide trailer that Frank had purchased for him, and perhaps out of loneliness and nostalgia for evenings spent in the company of Frank and Bessie, he sketched from memory on a roll of butcher paper the Dent family tree that his grandfather had shown to him many years before, and he studied it as if it were a book of wisdom. It was the numbers that drew him in, the birth and death dates, and the ruled lines that connected them, topmost twig to branch, branch to limb, limb to trunk, trunk to root.

He saw that alongside the names and birth and death dates of old Sam Dent and his direct descendants, there were branches and connectors without numbers and names attached. The lowermost branches, for instance, named for Sam Dent's four children who had predeceased him, were undated, and the line for Sam Dent's wife, Amelia, the half Mohawk whose father was rumored to have been a Catholic priest, had no dates. There were blank spaces for second, third, and fourth cousins, for his ancestors' unnamed and unnumbered siblings, aunts and uncles and their offspring.

Just below the topmost branch, Stevie's own mother's name, Amy Dent, was linked by a horizontal line to his father's, Chip Dent, with her date of birth, 1981, but no death date. Frank had told him that she, too, was distantly, if indirectly, descended from Sam Dent, but there were no names or dates for her parents or for the twigs and branches leading from her name back down the trunk to the root. These absences filled Stevie with a longing for completion that he knew would be satisfied only when he had named and dated all the blanks in his family tree and had drawn the lines that connected them, ultimately, to himself.

He remembered once clicking onto a website in response to an online advertisement from a company named 23andMe that promised *"Ancestry Breakdown . . . Dig deeper into your ancestry . . . the most complete genetic breakdown on the market, and the most comprehensive portrait of you yet."* He was attracted not to the product, which cost ninety-nine dollars, but to the name, 23andMe. 23andMe was more or less how Stevie thought of himself, a number, 23, linked to a personal pronoun, me. His surging interest in filling in the blanks in his family tree had led him to the 23andMe link, and he filled out the application form and paid the fee with his debit card and waited for the arrival of the kit that would collect his DNA and open the portal to his ancestry.

A week later he spit into a tube and as instructed mailed in the tube, and two weeks after that was notified online that his personalized Ancestry Report and a Relatives List were now available. He logged in and was told that he was 99.3% Northwestern European, 93.9% of which was British and Irish. He was also 0.5% Indigenous American and 0.2% African. None of this data particularly interested or surprised him.

He clicked on over to the tab for Family Tree and prepared to transfer the data from the 23andMe chart onto his grandfather's paper chart. The 23andMe diagram was less a standing tree like his grandfather's than a cluster of brightly colored balloons of different sizes and colors tied to long looping strings held in an invisible child's hand. Lines squiggled right and left, up and down and away, as if originating in the big yellow circle at the center, the one with his initials, *SD*, and below it his name, *Steven Dent*. A slightly smaller red circle floated just above his, with the letters *AD* on it and beneath the circle the word *Mother* and her name, his birth mother's name, *Amy Dent*, the most significant name in his ancestry. No dates, no numbers, however. Which meant that she was alive! Through the magic of 23andMe, his mother, from somewhere in the digital ether, was reaching out to him!

There was a dropdown menu that invited him to contact her by email. He typed, *I think I'm your son Stevie. Are you my mother?*

Within an hour he had his answer. *Yes, I am your mother.*

He wrote back, *Where are you?*

Her answer came at once. *Plattsburgh, New York.*

I'm in Sam Dent, just 40 miles away! Can we meet up?

Are you mad at me? Do you forgive me for being a bad mommy and leaving you with Frank and Bessie when you were a little kid?

Their emails went on into the night and increased in length and degree of delight and intimacy. She confessed to having been "in a bad head" after Stevie's dad was killed in Iraq. She knew that Frank and Bessie would take better care of him than she could have back then. She said that she "made some poor decisions and got in with a bad crowd" and thought it was best for him and everyone else if she just left town. She had indeed gone off to Florida with a "no-good man." Eventually she got free of him and came back to the area. She had been living in Plattsburgh for close to three years now, but didn't dare show up in Sam Dent, she said, because of the circumstances surrounding her departure. Also, she was sure that Frank and Bessie hated her and wouldn't allow her to see Stevie.

Stevie thought she was right about that. But he was old enough now to make his own decisions about who to see and who to avoid. He wanted to arrange a meeting with her. Frank and Bessie didn't need to know about it. He had a truck, and tomorrow after work he could drive up to Platts-burgh and meet her there.

And so, at a McDonald's in Plattsburgh just off the North-way at Exit 37, Stevie Dent, at the age of twenty, for the first time since he was five years old, sat down face-to-face with his mother. I need not say that it was a momentous meet-ing for both. Of course it was.

They embraced, a little tentatively at first, then with happy enthusiasm. Stevie had come straight from work at the greenhouse and wore his work clothes, a Willow Wood T-shirt and jeans and battered New York Yankees baseball cap. Amy was a small woman, shorter even than Stevie, but muscular with ropy veins on her tattooed arms and hands. She wore a faded black Megadeth tee and black jeans and high-top sneakers. Her hair, mouse brown with dyed lav-ender streaks, was chopped off short, as if she'd cut it her-self without a mirror. Her ears were unusually large for so small a person and laced with double rows of silver rings and studs.

Stevie's memory of her was sharp, even though he'd last

seen her fifteen years ago, when he was a very small boy, but in his eyes she had not changed, nor had he. To him their relative sizes were the same now as they were then—she was a towering adult woman, as powerful and all-knowing as a Greek goddess, and he was a child, tiny and weak and ignorant of everything in the world that mattered. She was as beautiful as a movie star, a different order of human being than he. She was an angel who could read his thoughts, and though he could not read hers, he knew that she loved him for his and did not hold his frail dependency and ignorance against him. He trusted her completely, the way he trusted Frank and Bessie. For the first time in his life, because he loved her, Stevie believed that he could love someone other than his grandparents.

They both ordered double Quarter Pounders with fries and Dr Peppers, and when they had finished eating, they stayed at their corner table and talked until late in the night. She told him everything that she liked and disliked, from food to cars to TV shows to music, without telling him what she did for a living or if she lived with anyone or if Stevie had a half brother or half sister or why she had spent ninety-nine dollars to register her DNA with 23andMe. He didn't ask about these things.

Mostly, when she wasn't enumerating her tastes and personal preferences, she asked him leading questions, and the questions kept him talking and her listening with nods and smiles as he unspooled the small events and episodes of his life with his grandparents at their old house in town and their new house on Irish Hill. He described his work at the greenhouse and the single-wide mobile home that his grandfather had bought for him and his Ford F-150 pickup truck.

At eleven they were told by the manager to order more food or leave. Outside, they stood beside his truck and continued talking, first one, usually a question from her, then the other, his answer. It was chilly, and she had put on a gray cotton hoodie and had pulled the hood over her head. Finally, the lights in the McDonald's parking lot went out. Amy patted Stevie's shoulder and said she had to leave and told him he should get back to Sam Dent. It was a long drive and he had work tomorrow, she reminded him. Like a mother. They hugged, and she stepped away and smiled and asked Stevie if he ever took a day off from his job.

He said yes, he had Sundays and Mondays off.

She said, "Stevie, I wonder if next Sunday you'd do me a huge favor."

He said, "Sure. Anything you want." He had an odd way of speaking, without inflection or variety of tone, regardless of content or context. He sounded like someone reading from a script, not for effect, but checking it aloud for errors in spelling and punctuation. Local folks made fun of his way of speaking, and a few, myself included, could do a fair imitation of it.

"Have you ever driven up to Canada, honey?"

"I don't think so."

"I need someone to drive me up to get a present a Canadian friend has for me. I don't trust that old bucket of rust to make it up and back," she said and nodded in the direction of the dark green ten-year-old Subaru Forester parked next to his truck. She explained that her friend lived close to the border, and the present was a new experimental medicine for her chronic back pain. The medicine was legal in Canada, but not in the United States, because it hadn't been approved yet by the FDA. "It's like this incredible miracle drug, but Big Pharma doesn't want it available here until they can control the patent and get Medicare to pay, like, ten thousand bucks a pop for it."

He said, "That doesn't seem right. I have good health insurance, you know. Because of my job," he added.

"Lucky you, honey. I don't have a job right now and can't afford Obamacare or qualify for Medicaid on account of I have a little trust fund my parents left me, which I don't want to give up. I keep it so I can pass it on to you someday. So no health insurance for little Amy. Thank you, President Barack Hussein Obama. Anyhow, we can't tell the customs guys at the border that we're bringing this medicine down for your mom, or they'll impound it and might bust us to make an example of us. The American government hates it that Canada has socialized medicine and we can buy prescription drugs cheaper there than here. But you don't have to worry. About getting busted, I mean. My friend'll show you how to hide it under your truck."

He said he understood. "Socialized medicine. Yeah, Obamacare. That's why me and Frank and Bessie, we all voted for Donald Trump. First time I ever voted, too."

"Good for you, hon. Make America great again. Trump might be a bastard, but he's *our* bastard, right?"

"Right."

She said that when she got home she'd call her friend Denis and tell him to expect her and Stevie to show up next Sunday afternoon. She explained that all they needed to cross the border was their New York driver's licenses. If the customs guys asked why they were going to Canada, he should say it was to visit a friend who was sick with cancer and they'd be returning to the States in a few hours. He could drop her off at her place when they got back, and they'd meet up later in Sam Dent. He could show her his trailer, and she could get her medicine from where it was hidden under his truck, and they could go out for supper together at the old Spread Eagle and celebrate over a couple of beers. "The Spread's still there, isn't it?"

"Yes, sure. Me and Frank and Bessie, we go for supper at the Spread Eagle sometimes, usually early, on account of it gets loud later and Frank and Bessie are Christians."

"Cool," she said. "I used to spend a whole lotta time there. Me and your dad. Probably a whole different crowd now," she added. "We can celebrate, and maybe you'll introduce me around."

"Yes, I will," he said. "What will we be celebrating?"

"Finding each other after all these years, hon! It's a mother and child reunion," she said and pinched his cheek. She spun away from him and wearing a wide smile danced over to her rusted-out Forester, singing the old Paul Simon song,

> But the mother and child reunion
> Is only a motion away . . .

The trip to Granby, a city of fifty thousand located halfway between Montreal and Sherbrooke in the Eastern Townships, went exactly as Amy planned. Before they got to the border, she removed all but one pair of her earrings and studs and put on a long-sleeved denim shirt to cover her black hand-drawn tattoos—barbed wire cuffs, four dots in a square with a single dot in the center on her forearms, matching teardrops on the underside of each wrist, and on the upper arms a snake's head and a spider web. At the border both the Canadian and American customs officers would have recognized them as jailhouse tattoos, triggering a lengthy interrogation and a thorough search of Stevie's F-150. Instead, the Canadians waved the young White woman and her son into their country, and five hours later the Americans welcomed them back.

In Granby, Denis and his friend Paul met them at their garage. It was an auto repair shop situated next to the Autodrome, a large dirt track where every Friday night from May to September drivers brought their modified stock cars from all over Quebec to race one another for trophies and ribbons and small cash prizes. Denis and Paul had two dogs on chained collars, a German shepherd that belonged to Denis and an English bulldog that was Paul's, and while Amy discussed the terms of her transaction with the two men in their office, Stevie hung out in the yard with the dogs. "They're watchdogs, not guard dogs," Paul had explained. "There's a difference."

"What's the difference?" Stevie asked.

"Watchdogs are all bark and no bite," he said and laughed. "Guard dogs are all bite and no bark."

While Stevie played with the dogs, Denis and Paul put his truck on a lift and wired a wide, flat, aluminum briefcase to the undercarriage between the leaf springs and the deck of the bed. No money changed hands. Over the past three years Amy had established a line of credit with Denis and Paul by retailing prepaid small-load marijuana and opioids to college students at Plattsburgh State. They were willing this time to advance her five kilos of crack cocaine for ninety days at $100 a gram. They had obtained it for $70 a gram from a member of the notorious West End biker gang in Montreal. Amy had convinced Denis that she could move crack quickly at twice her cost in the small towns and villages of upstate New York. The region was too far north of New York City and New Jersey and southern New England to attract competitors, street dealers who'd likely be Black or Hispanic and up there would get busted just for the color of their skin. She, by contrast, was a thirty-nine-year-old white woman, a local. You'd expect to see her working the night shift behind the counter at a Stewart's selling lotto tickets and coffee to truck drivers.

The West End Gang was eager to break into that untapped upstate New York market, and Amy Dent, Denis's and Paul's small-time weed and pill dealer in Plattsburgh, was a possible entry point. Like bankers buying and reselling mortgages, just as Denis and Paul had taken a chance on Amy, the West End Gang had taken a chance on Denis and Paul. No one was sure how this kid Stevie fit in, but Amy said he was her son, and he knew all the locals personally and was the last person anyone down there would think was dealing.

Driving back from Granby, Stevie asked Amy, "Did you sign up for 23andMe so you could get in touch with me?

You could've just called me on the phone and saved ninety-nine dollars."

"I would have called, but I asked around and found out you were living with Frank and Bessie, and I knew they didn't want me seeing you."

"So how come you signed up for 23andMe?"

They were approaching the U.S. border crossing, and she was anxious about that and didn't answer right away. It was late afternoon, and a pile of dark clouds was moving north toward them, obscuring their view of the Adirondack Mountains. The customs officer, a fifty-something white man with military bearing, asked them where they had been in Canada and how long and why, and they mostly told the truth. He asked Stevie where he lived, and Stevie said, "Sam Dent, New York."

"You sure?" He took a second long look at Stevie's and Amy's driver's licenses. "Your last names, they're the same as where you say you live," he said. "Dent." He looked like he was about to tell them to get out of the truck and step into the office for questioning.

Stevie started, "I think it's because—"

"We're descended from the guy the town's named after," Amy said.

"Interesting," the officer said. "So there was a real Sam Dent. I always wondered about the name of that town. Okay, go ahead," he said and returned their licenses and waved them through.

They were silent for a few miles, until it began to rain, and Amy said, "Yeah, Sam Dent. That's why I registered on 23andMe. The man, I mean. My parents' last name was Clarkson, but when I married your dad they said him and me were distantly related, like third or fourth cousins. One of my great-great-grandfathers was named Sam Dent, they said. They were worried about me marrying another Dent and having his kid. So I wanted to check it out."

"Why were they worried about you marrying a Dent and having his kid?"

"You're not supposed to have kids with relatives. In case there's a bad gene on both sides that gets doubled in the kid and causes deformities like eleven toes or inherited ill-nesses like Alzheimer's."

"Oh. Were you worried about marrying a Dent like my dad and having his kid?"

"No," she said. "Just curious."

"His kid, that would be me."

"Right."

"So it was like an accident that we both signed up for 23andMe and found each other that way."

"Right."

"So it was an accidental mother and son reunion."

"Right."

Ninety-seven days later—the morning of the night that Frank and Bessie were kidnapped and smuggled like refu-gees into Canada—Denis and Paul crossed into the U.S., looking for Amy and their $100 a gram, plus whatever was left of the five kilos of crack cocaine they had advanced her. The West End Gang had sent a delegation to Granby to col-lect and had pointed guns at Denis's and Paul's heads and had given them forty-eight hours to come up with $350,000 in U.S. cash or the equivalent in unsold crack cocaine. To make their point, they shot Denis's German shepherd and Paul's English bulldog with a single bullet to the brain of each dog. It made a strong impression on Denis and Paul.

For weeks Denis had been trying to check in with Amy, but she had not picked up. Her voicemail box was full and was no longer accepting messages.

Paul said, "You don't think the bitch and the kid left town with the rock, do you? Like to another state."

Denis, who was proud of having a photographic memory, remembered Stevie's name and his Willow Wood Nursery T-shirt. He looked up the nursery website and called and asked for Steve Dent. The man who answered, Benny Brown, said Stevie was off on Fridays and was probably at home and gave him Stevie's number.

Stevie answered at once. Denis said he was his mom's friend from Granby up in Canada, and Stevie said, "Oh."

"You remember me?"

"Yes."

Denis explained that he was trying to reach Stevie's mom, but she wasn't picking up and her phone mailbox was full.

Stevie said, "Oh."

"So how can I get in touch with her? I need to talk to her."

"She's mostly at her place in Plattsburgh, I guess."

"She hasn't left town or anything, has she?"

"No."

Denis said maybe he'd take a drive down to meet her in Plattsburgh. He wondered if Stevie had her address.

"Yeah."

"Well, can you give it to me?"

"422 Hamilton Street. Apartment 3F."

Denis said thanks and asked Stevie not to mention he was coming down to see her. He was bringing a present and wanted it to be a surprise.

Stevie said, "Are you my mother's boyfriend?"

"You could kinda say that."

"She was married to my dad. He got killed in Iraq. But she's not married now," he said. "So I guess it's okay that you're her boyfriend."

"Thanks, kid. That's real sweet of you. Sorry about your dad, though."

Stevie said it was okay, it happened a long time ago.

In his best American accent, Denis said they were from NYSEG, checking out a report of a gas leak in the building. Amy unlocked the door and let the two men into her apartment. She realized her mistake at once. She rushed into the bedroom where she kept her Glock 19, but they grabbed her by the arms before she reached it and threw her onto the unmade bed. Denis held her hands while Paul yanked the pillowcase off one of the pillows and pulled it over her head. They wore matching tan pigskin gloves and carried pistols and had brought a roll of duct tape that they used to bind her wrists and ankles and tighten the pillowcase around her neck.

The television was tuned to a *Dr. Phil* episode—"The Six

Quickest Ways to Ruin a Marriage." Denis cranked up the volume, and he and Paul proceeded to ransack the dark, cluttered apartment. They pawed through the drawers and cabinets, the closets and suitcases and shoeboxes and canisters, pulling and shaking everything out, clothes, linens, pots and pans, emptying jars and cans into the sink and onto counters, dumping the contents of cupboards and the freezer and refrigerator onto the linoleum floor.

Amy sat on the bed, bound and in darkness, saying nothing. She knew what they were after and what they were doing and what was going to happen next. It took longer for them to give up the search than she expected, but finally she felt the weight of them as they sat down on the bed on either side of her. Dr. Phil was still opining in the living room. Denis leaned in close to her covered head and said she had one chance to tell them where she had stashed the cash and the remainder of the crack they had advanced her.

Paul said, "The bitch's a fucking clucker. She probably burned it all herself."

Denis said, "That true?"

"No. I didn't touch the stuff. And I didn't deal any of it. I didn't want to tell you. I was scared to tell you . . . that I changed my mind. About dealing, I mean."

Denis said, "So where the fuck is it, then?"

"I didn't know how to get it back to you. I couldn't mail it, obviously. And on account of Trump, there's ICE agents and National Guard units covering the border now. Nobody gets in or out without their vehicle getting searched top to bottom. It's not like it used to be, crossing the border. I didn't know what to do with the stuff."

Denis asked again, "So where the fuck is it? Since you suddenly got a conscience about dealing and didn't smoke it yourself."

She was silent for a few seconds. She heard the click of the safety on a pistol being released. She thought she could smell the lubricant used to clean the weapon. It smelled like rubber-cement glue. She said, "It's still where you put it. When we were up in Granby."

"In the truck?" Paul said. "Under the kid's truck?"

"Yeah. He's the reason I changed my mind about dealing. I didn't want Stevie involved. He's only a kid, for chrissakes. He doesn't know what's in the briefcase. He thinks it was medicine for my back. He's probably forgotten it's even there."

"Where's his truck?" Paul asked.

"In Sam Dent. He lives there."

"What's the address?"

"I don't know."

"The fuck you don't know."

"Please, promise you won't hurt him! He's a sweet kid."

Denis said, "We won't hurt him. We just want that briefcase and the rock inside. If it's still there, no problem. If it's not there, yes, Amy, big problem."

She said, "It'll be under his truck where you put it."

"So where's the fucking truck?"

She hesitated for a few seconds. "He's got a single-wide trailer on Route 9N. It's at the top of Spruce Hill on the left coming from Elizabethtown. I don't know the exact number."

She felt their weight leave the bed and knew they were

standing over her. She could hear them breathing. One of them had a cold. That was the last thing she knew. They both shot her once in the head at close range. Two bullets. The pillowcase kept the blood and brain matter from spattering them. With Dr. Phil still loudly explaining the six quickest ways to ruin a marriage, they left the apartment and got into Denis's pickup and drove forty miles south into the valley between the mountains to the village of Sam Dent.

We later learned that Stevie was aware of more than his mother gave him credit for. He was odd, but not stupid. He had not forgotten the aluminum briefcase that Denis and Paul had attached to the underside of his truck. And he understood that the briefcase was filled with illegal drugs, not Canadian medicine for his mother's back. He had left it there, untouched, wired to the chassis between the leaf springs and the truck bed, and over the summer neither he nor his mother had mentioned its existence, though they talked often together by phone and saw each other in Sam Dent every few weeks when she drove down to hang out at the Spread Eagle with him and her old and new friends. The briefcase filled with crack was a subject they could not yet broach, though both knew that eventually they would.

We in town could see that during those months Amy Dent was creating a new life for herself. In a sense she was at the same time creating a new life for Stevie. She was unemployed, but received enough income from the trust left by her parents to cover her rent and other living expenses, around $2,500 a month. Prior to that summer she had been dealing small quantities of party drugs in Plattsburgh, mainly as a way to satisfy her own cravings and to boost her social life. But most of her customers were in their early twenties and late teens, and she was approaching forty. She was starting to feel too old to be getting high with college students. She still smoked grass on a daily basis, but had given up pills and speed and cocaine. She probably drank a little too much, but was careful not to start before five o'clock, and she mainly stuck to beer. At the Spread Eagle with Stevie she liked flirting with the local married guys she had known in high school, and she had sex with a couple of them in their cars and pickup trucks in the parking lot out back. She was even thinking of moving back to Sam Dent and trying to make amends with Frank and Bessie and maybe sharing a place with her son, swapping out his single-wide for a double-wide. Reuniting with her lost and abandoned son on 23andMe had given her the first chance since the death of Stevie's father to remake her life. Agreeing to deal crack for Denis and Paul now looked like a bad decision. Something the old Amy would do, not the new. But because of President Trump's immigration policy, which she basically supported, she hadn't yet figured out how to get the crack safely back to the Canadians without involving Stevie, and then Denis and Paul came to her apartment in Plattsburgh and shot her.

When Stevie arrived at work and learned about Denis's phone call that morning, he wasn't initially alarmed. But a few hours later, he was lugging a dozen potted young Japanese maples on a cart from the greenhouse to the outdoor nursery to give them space to spread their delicate branches and filigreed red leaves, and it occurred to him that when Denis said he was his mother's boyfriend he hadn't told the truth. The guy didn't even know where she lived. How could he be her boyfriend? That he was lying relieved Stevie. He didn't want his mother to have a boyfriend, especially a Canadian guy who was probably a drug dealer. Then he wished he hadn't given Denis his mother's address. If Denis wasn't her boyfriend, then he must have been looking for the money she owed him for whatever was in the briefcase.

Stevie decided he should warn her. He tried calling her cellphone, but she didn't pick up. Her mailbox was not taking messages. The Canadian guy had told the truth about that much, anyhow. He walked to the office and asked his boss, Benny Brown, if he could leave early. He said he had a migraine. He wasn't sure what a migraine was, but he had seen a TV ad for Motrin Liquid Gels demonstrated by a woman suffering from one. To show Benny how much pain he was in, he twisted his face into a grimace like the woman in the ad. He said he had to pick up some Motrin Liquid Gels at the Kinney Pharmacy in Elizabethtown, and Bennie said sure, no problem. He left the nursery and drove instead to his trailer on Spruce Hill.

On his back he shimmied under the truck and with a pair of pliers loosened the wires binding the briefcase to the frame and worked the case free. He didn't open it. He placed it on the floor of the cab in front of the passenger seat, handling it carefully, as if it were a roadside bomb, like the IED that killed his dad. He got into the driver's seat and backed the truck onto Route 9N and headed north through the town of Ausable Forks, where the east and west branches of the Ausable River merge, and drove east along the thickened river's meandering route through Keeseville, twenty miles downstream.

In Precambrian times, the river cut a narrow gorge two hundred feet deep into the sandstone shelf on the far side of Keeseville. The gorge is now a tourist attraction called Ausable Chasm. The road crosses the chasm at its deepest point on a two-lane bridge, and over the years several spectacular suicides have occurred there. In one famous case not long ago, two women deliberately killed themselves and their four children by driving their van off the bridge into the churning waters below. Stevie knew the story. Everyone knew the story.

Stevie drove across the bridge and turned right and parked his truck in the public lot. He got out and walked around to the passenger's side and lifted the briefcase from the floor and carried it flat in both hands like an offering to an altar and walked out to the midpoint of the bridge on the downstream side. He stopped there for a few seconds, looked left and right and saw no one else on the bridge and no cars or trucks coming from either direction.

It was a late August afternoon. The azure sky was clear, and the bright green pine and cedar forests on the surrounding hills and the high sedimented sandstone cliffs and the rock-tumbled waters of the river below were bathed in soft golden sunlight. Stevie extended his arms above the chest-high guardrail like a priest and let the shiny aluminum briefcase slide off and down into the chasm. He leaned over the guardrail and watched it fall, watched it hit the water, where it went under for a second, watched it get tossed back to the surface by the roaring current, where it got sent swiftly downstream like a whitewater raft, spinning and swirling in the rapids around the distant bend in the river and out of sight. Stevie imagined it floating the last few miles to where the river empties into the deep, cold, slow-moving waters of Lake Champlain, west to east from New York to Vermont, 25 miles wide, and south to north from the United States into Canada, 125 miles long. He imagined the briefcase bobbing slowly northward on the low waves of the lake all the way to the outflow at the Richelieu River in Quebec and on to the wide St. Lawrence River east of Montreal. He imagined it caught by the strong northeastern current of the St. Lawrence, floating a thousand miles into the North Atlantic, where at last the battering of the storm-tossed waves would smash it open, fill it with sea water, and send the case and its contents to the icy dark bottom of the sea, and finally Stevie and his mother would be released from the curse and the burden of the thing.

He walked slowly back to his truck and tried calling his mother's phone one more time and got the same message, her mailbox was full. At Ausable Chasm he was already halfway to Plattsburgh, so he decided to drive on to her place and confess in person that he had stupidly given her address to Denis. It might anger her, but he felt he should warn her anyhow.

He pulled into the unpaved driveway beside the unkempt, peeling, three-story Victorian manse. The house had been converted decades ago into six small, badly maintained flats for single mothers and their kids and pensioners and transitory college students living off-campus. He parked next to Amy's green Forester, went in the front entrance and started up the stairs. On the second-floor landing a barefoot man in his fifties with a belly shaped like a melon, his gray-haired arms folded aggressively across his sunken chest, stood by the open door of his apartment. He wore a sleeveless T-shirt and floppy Bermuda shorts held up by suspenders. The smell of stale cigarette smoke and cold corned beef wafted from the apartment out to the narrow dark stairway.

"You goin' up to 3F?"

"Yes."

"Hear that? Of *course* you hear it."

"What?"

"The fuckin' TV! Tell her to turn her fuckin' TV down! I can't nap, I can't fuckin' read the paper, I can't fuckin' *think*! She won't open her door or answer me when I knock and try to tell her myself."

"Maybe she's not home."

"Door's not locked. I tried it, but I don't enter the home of a female without an invite. Not these days. She's in there all right, but she don't like me. Maybe she likes you. Does she like you?"

"I think so."

"Then tell her to turn her fuckin' TV down!" he shouted and stepped back inside his apartment and slammed the door and locked it.

Stevie made himself listen for a few seconds, and yes, he heard his mother's TV, and it was indeed very loud. It was tuned to *America's Got Talent*. As a child, so that he could think his own thoughts, Stevie had developed the habit of muffling loud or discordant sounds when people were talking nearby or the TV or radio was on. Otherwise, his thoughts got shattered and displaced by the noise, for that was all it was to him, noise. Listening to his mother's crabby neighbor and then the TV had made him briefly forget why he was in his mother's building. He was aware that he had never been here before. As he climbed the darkened stairs from the second-floor landing to the door of her apartment, he blocked the noise of *America's Got Talent* and welcomed his thoughts back and remembered again why he had come here.

He knocked softly and strained to hear through the blather of the TV. He said, "Mom? It's Stevie."

No answer. He tried the handle and pushed, and the door swung open. He picked up the remote from the floor and shut off the TV and gazed at the wreckage of the living room and kitchen and tried to imagine how his mother could live with such disorder. Like his grandparents, Stevie was compulsively neat and orderly. Anything out of alignment or set at a wrong angle or not in its proper place made him anxious and kept him agitated until he was able to set it right. He started to shut the open kitchen drawers and close the cabinet doors, and remembered again why he was here.

"Mom?" he called out. "Are you home, Mom?"

There were three doors off the sparsely furnished living room, two open and one closed. The first was to a coat closet that had its contents tossed onto the floor. A second led to a bathroom. He peeked in and saw the medicine cabinet with half its contents dumped into the sink. The third door was closed. He supposed it led to her bedroom and she was on the other side of it, asleep or, more likely, passed out, or else she would have been wakened by the TV or by the crabby neighbor or by Stevie's knock and call. He knew that she smoked a lot of grass and thought she drank too much. He himself did not smoke pot or drink, because he got dizzy and confused from just one toke or a single glass of beer. He knocked softly and said, "Mom?"

He pushed on the door, and it swung open. There was a woman's tiny body lying on the bed. He saw that her wrists and ankles and the pillowcase over her head were bound with duct tape. The pillowcase and the bedding were soaked with blood. He stared and did not move toward her. He had never seen a dead body before. He felt ashamed and embarrassed, as if he had walked in on the woman and had caught her without any clothes on. She was very small, smaller than he, so he knew it was not his mother, who he knew was much larger than he. He had never seen a woman's unclothed body before, and though he had long wanted to see one, he was glad it was not his mother's and that she was wearing clothes. He wondered who she was. Though she was dead and not naked, he wanted to apologize for having caught her unawares like this.

He suddenly realized that his cellphone was ringing. After the third ring he drew the phone from his pocket, and looked at the screen and saw that his grandfather was calling him. He touched *Answer* and said, "Hey, Pops, wussup."

Frank said, "Stevie, there's someone here wants . . ."

A different person spoke, and Stevie recognized Denis's voice and the French accent. It was his mother's Canadian boyfriend. "I got your fucking grandparents here, Steve! You want to see them alive again, you know what you gotta do." Stevie stared at the screen for a few seconds, then glanced over at the woman's body on the bed.

"Steve? This is Denis, Steve."

Stevie pressed the Home button on his phone and ended the call. He backed out of his mother's bedroom and shut the door and quickly left the apartment and started down the stairs. At the second-floor landing, he passed the burly neighbor standing in the open doorway of his apartment, smoking a cigarette. Without meeting his gaze Stevie slowed and walked by.

The man said, "You got the magic touch, kid."

"I do?"

"Yeah, the fuckin' TV. You got her to shut it off. Thanks."

"You're welcome."

"I guess she likes 'em young. You ain't the only kid marching up and down them stairs, y' know."

"I'm not?"

"None of my business, but what the fuck's she selling up there? Drugs? Sex, maybe? Not that I give a damn, as long as she keeps the noise down."

Stevie nodded but said nothing and continued down the stairs and out. He crossed the rutted driveway and got into his truck. He tried to think of where to go now and what to do when he got there. It was almost dark. He noticed that his legs felt watery and his hands were trembling. There was a wind roaring in his ears that kept him from thinking anything. He sat behind the steering wheel of his truck waiting for the wind to die down, and he didn't start the engine for a long time.

Then it was dark, and a few hours later the lone Canadian officer at the Customs and Border Protection post in Champlain, New York, waved Denis back into Canada. He drove northeast on Route 221 for a half mile, then turned east onto a flat mesh of back roads, past truck and dairy farms into the township of Lacolle, where at the side of an unpaved country lane he met up with his partner and their captives. Paul and Bessie took their seats in back as before, and Denis and Frank sat in the front. Denis and Paul exchanged a few words in French, and a minute later they were headed north again.

Paul offered Frank and Bessie a beer and some Cheetos. Bessie just shook her head no and looked down at her hands folded in her lap like she was about to cry or pray.

Frank said, "Sure, why not?" and cracked open the warm can of Budweiser and grabbed a handful of Cheetos from the bag. He drank and ate and looked out the windshield at the dark starry sky passing overhead and wondered why Stevie was hiding from these two men and what exactly did he owe them. It had to do with selling drugs, he knew that much, but how on earth did their Stevie end up selling drugs? Their Stevie was a good boy, and these two were bad men. Their Stevie had no need for money, other than his weekly pay from the Willow Wood plant nursery. His home and truck were paid for. He liked his job, and the folks who ran the nursery, Benny and Cecilia Brown, valued him and had made his position more or less permanent and year-round and were even paying for half his health insurance. The only other year-round permanent position with benefits available to a recent high school graduate from Sam Dent was to guard the mostly Black and Hispanic inmates in one of the numerous federal and state prisons in Essex and Clinton Counties—brutal, soul-crushing work that turned good kids like Stevie into burnt-out sadists. Frank knew of many such cases.

But Stevie, because of his grandparents, was lucky, and Frank believed that when God has made you lucky, you make plans and decisions that will preserve and exploit your luck. You don't get involved with men like Denis and Paul and start selling drugs in your hometown to the people you went to high school with. And if along the way you do make a bad decision and you get involved with men like Denis and Paul, you don't try to cheat them so they end up kidnapping your grandparents in order to get back what you owe them. For the first time since he and Bessie had brought little Stevie to live with them in their home and Bessie quit her job at the bank in order to raise him, Frank wished that he and Bessie had left the child with his mother, or barring that, had given him over to one of those state-run foster care agencies. The wish flashed past, and he felt his brain tighten like a fist, and he didn't think it again.

It took them little over an hour to reach the garage in Granby. Denis pulled up to the three-bay door, and Paul got out and unlocked and raised the middle door and Denis drove the truck inside. Paul brought the door down and locked it and flipped on the overhead fluorescent lights. Together he and Denis marched Frank and Bessie and their suitcase from the truck to a small windowless storage room at the rear of the garage. Frank put down their suitcase, and Denis, like a hotel porter, showed them the closet-sized lavatory with a toilet and small sink. The couple stood waiting, as if wondering how much to tip him. Paul dragged in a double mattress and flopped it on the concrete floor against one of the unpainted cinderblock walls, and Denis filled a gallon plastic jug with water from the lavatory sink and handed it to Frank, who thanked him.

Denis said, "You're probably hungry."

Bessie scowled and crossed her arms defiantly over her chest and said, "Now, you listen here, mister—" but Frank interrupted and said, "Yes, we could use something to eat." He had decided to be as cooperative and unthreatening as possible, to behave as if they were here of their own volition. He hoped he could trick the men into thinking that he and Bessie would not try to escape, so they could somehow slip away from the garage and go straight to the police. He wondered if Canada still used Mounties for policing and if the Mounties had a station house in Granby.

Denis checked his watch and said, "Pizza Hut is still open. Pizza okay?"

Frank smiled and said, "Sure. With pepperoni."

Denis pulled out his cellphone and called Pizza Hut and ordered delivery of a large pepperoni pizza.

Frank said, "What about my phone? I'd like it back, if

you don't mind. I can't call anyone from Canada, you know. I can only use it in the States. It's a Verizon account, and I don't have international calling. No texting or emailing, either."

Denis flashed a thin-lipped smile below his mustache and shook his head, as if a little disgusted by the request. "So why do you need it for, Pepé?" he said and laughed. "You probably want your guns back, too. And your passports and driver's licenses." Then he and Paul, laughing, left the room and shut the door behind them and locked it.

Frank and Bessie looked around and silently inventoried the sparse contents of the pale, windowless room. There was a single overhead fluorescent shop light but no visible wall switch. Besides the mattress on the floor and their suitcase, there were two cardboard boxes of Valvoline motor oil and a wooden pallet with nothing on it, and a pair of tires—racing slicks—and four encrusted twelve-volt car batteries that looked dead, stashed for recycling.

So these two actually were auto mechanics and ran what appeared to be a legitimate business, Frank thought. They weren't just drug dealers and kidnappers. He found that encouraging. Frank and Bessie couldn't have known it at the time, but we learned later from news accounts and testimony at the trial that Denis and Paul shared the large apartment above the garage. The building itself was more than a century old, the first regional assembly plant for Ford Model T cars. Both men had arrest records and had served time in prison, Denis for writing bad checks and nonpayment of child support, Paul for assault. Denis was alcoholic, and Paul consumed large daily doses of testosterone. The men were not lovers, or so we assumed. Denis was divorced with three young children he hadn't seen in two years who were living with his ex-wife in Sherbrooke. Paul, who had never married, was known in Granby for his sexual prowess and kept himself busy servicing a string of three or four local women at a time. It was a compulsion, like his weight lifting, not romance or even sex.

Frank's initial estimation of them as clowns, too stupid to be dangerous, wasn't altogether wrong. But because of their stupidity, they were indeed dangerous. For instance, it had not been in their long-range interest to shoot Amy Dent, but they did it anyway. They didn't think of themselves as psychopathic killers. They were merely imitating the American gangsters they admired in American films directed by people like Martin Scorsese and Quentin Tarantino and the Coen brothers and TV shows like *The Sopranos*—they had been angry and scared of the West End Gang and happened to have guns in their hands, and Amy had not delivered what she promised, so they shot her. Now, because they couldn't locate Amy's presumed accomplice, they had this kidnapped elderly American couple on their hands. It hadn't occurred to them yet, but they were probably going to have to shoot them, too.

Also, without knowing it, Denis and Paul were caught in an off-the-books financial trap. For the moment, the elderly American couple was their only asset, their collateral, in what they correctly viewed as a strictly financial relationship at one end between themselves and the West End Gang and at the other between themselves and the American woman, Amy Dent. It was the same as the relationship between any

large bank and a smaller one, between any lender and bor-
rower. Except that compliance with the terms of the loan
was enforced not by government regulation or the courts,
but by the threat of personalized violence, starting with
the murder of the borrowers' watchdogs by the West End
Gang and moving on down the chain of the loan to Amy
and on to Stevie, Amy's accomplice who she claimed was
her son. If the Canadians couldn't get their collateral from
Stevie, then they were stuck with Frank and Bessie. In the
end, somebody had to pay, because in the end everybody
has to pay.

Bessie started to cry, and Frank hugged her and patted
her shuddering shoulders. He told her to pray to Jesus. As
if afraid the room was bugged, he whispered in her ear. "We
mustn't panic, sweetheart. We have to act like this is just
a temporary inconvenience for us, so they'll relax and let
their guard down. That's my plan."

"Your plan," she said. "You and your plans, Frank."

"Just keep praying to Jesus. You don't like my plan, ask
Him to come up with a better one."

"The Lord will save us. He won't let these awful men
hurt us, will He?"

"No."

A half hour later, Denis brought them the pepperoni
pizza and set it on the floor near where Bessie and Frank
were seated on the mattress. He said, "Pepé, you told me a
fucking lie. You lied about your fucking phone."

Paul stood glowering by the door, his meat-packed arms
crossed over his enormous chest. He bounced on his toes,
as if preparing to run across the room and attack the elderly
couple.

Frank calmly handed Bessie a slice of pizza and took another for himself. "I did?"

"I just tested it. I used your phone to call the number of a friend, a woman down in Plattsburgh. The call went through fine, no problem. I'd have left her a message, but her mailbox is full. So you do have international calling on this phone, Pepé. If I'd left it with you, like you asked, you could've really fucked things up for us."

Frank explained that he had never been able to make heads or tails of his Verizon bill. He had never ordered international calling, so had just assumed he wasn't signed up for it. "They do that, you know, charge you for service you never asked for. And since you rarely use it and it's not itemized on your bill, you don't know you have it. I'll call Verizon in the morning and get them to take it off my account," he said.

Denis laughed. "Yeah, right. You do that. Before you do anything, though, we got to call your grandson, Steve."

Bessie said, "What? No, leave Stevie alone! It's his mother, it's Amy, she's the one who dragged him into this somehow. He's got nothing to do with your drug business!"

Frank shushed her by raising the flat of his hand. He said to Denis, "If Stevie is trying to hide from you, he may not answer."

"He'll take a call from his grandpa. Put the phone on speaker so I can hear. Tell him he needs to deliver the briefcase and its contents that we gave him and his mother back in May, or we'll do to his grandparents what we did to his mother. Say that. I won't talk this time. Just you talk. Paul might have to slap the old lady a couple times to make her scream in the background, so little Stevie knows we are not fucking around. But you do the talking, Pepé. You're smart, you can convince him to bring us the briefcase."

Her voice breaking, Bessie said, "What . . . what did you do to Stevie's mother?"

Paul barked a laugh and said, "*Mamie*, believe me, you don't want to know."

Frank said, "Leave Bessie alone. Please, just leave her alone. I'll tell Stevie to do whatever you want. He does what I say. He always does what I say. He's a good boy."

Denis passed Frank's phone over to him, and Frank put it on speaker and punched in Stevie's number.

Stevie was sitting in his grandfather's La-Z-Boy chair, watching the local late news from Plattsburgh on Frank and Bessie's big-screen high-definition TV. Sixty-four inches! He loved that TV and had urged them for months to buy it, until finally, over Bessie's objections, Frank had driven up to Walmart in Plattsburgh with Stevie and bought it and gave Stevie their old thirty-two-inch flat-screen TV for his trailer. Tonight's top story was the discovery of the body of a murdered woman in a Plattsburgh apartment building. Her identity was being withheld, pending notification of next of kin. Her death by gunshot wounds to the head was thought to be drug-related.

On the first ring of the phone Stevie muted the TV. "Hello?" he said, as if he didn't know who was calling. But he did. He could see the number of the caller on the screen, his grandfather's. Almost no one else called him, except his mother. Today was unusual—three phone calls in twelve hours. There was the Canadian guy this morning who said he was Stevie's mother's boyfriend and wanted her address.

Then later the call from his grandfather's phone when the same Canadian guy yelled at him, so he hung up. And now here was his grandfather again. It was after eleven, late for his grandfather to be calling. "Is that you, Pops?"

Frank said, "Yes, Stevie, it's me."

"Oh. Wussup? Where are you? I'm at your house on Irish Hill, but nobody's here. Your car's here, but you and Grandma aren't."

"That's right, Stevie. We're in Canada. See, we've been sort of kidnapped, your grandma and me. And they won't let us go, unless you do something for them. Do you understand?"

"Sure. You mean the kidnappers? What do they want me to do?"

"They want you to return the briefcase and its contents that they gave you and Amy back in May."

"Oh."

Frank said, "So you know about the briefcase and its contents?"

"Sure. They wired it to the frame under my truck, so me and my mom could bring it from Canada."

"Well, they want it back, Stevie. They're deadly serious, these men. You have to give it back."

"I can't."

"What do you mean, you can't?" Frank looked up at Denis, who stood over him, his face iced with anger.

"I got rid of it. The briefcase. And what was inside."

Bessie cried, "Oh, dear God, Stevie! Don't say that! What did you do with it?"

Stevie said, "Hi, Grandma. Are you okay?"

In as calm and steady a voice as he could manage, Frank said, "Tell us what you did with the briefcase, Stevie." He felt like he was negotiating in a crowded mall with a terrorist wearing a suicide vest.

"I guess I should've kept it. I didn't know they'd kidnap you guys and use you for ransom."

"Tell us what you did with the briefcase, Stevie," Frank said again. "Maybe we can get it back."

"No, you can't. I dropped it into the river from the bridge at Ausable Chasm. It floated real good. It's probably in the ocean by now. The Ausable River empties into Lake Champlain, you know, and the lake connects to the St. Lawrence River, and the St. Lawrence flows to the ocean. It's gone. Unless it ends up in Europe someday," he said and laughed.

"Oh, Jesus," Frank said softly. "Oh, sweet Jesus."

In the background Bessie started to weep. Stevie heard her and said, "Don't cry, Grandma. They can't get what they want now, so they'll just have to let you and Pops come home. Or if you need a ride, I can drive up and get you. I remember where it is from when I was there with my mother that other time."

"Don't do that, Stevie! Stay away from here!" Frank yelled.

Denis grabbed the phone from Frank and clicked off. "That idiot! That fucking idiot! He threw the briefcase into the fucking river!"

Paul spoke a few quick sentences in French, and Denis shook his head slowly in response and said, *"Pourquoi pas?"*

Bessie rubbed her hands as if they'd been scalded. Frank slumped back onto the mattress and stared at the ceiling. He looked like he had been wakened suddenly from a long night's deep sleep and didn't yet recognize the room he was in.

Had we known the story to this point, we would not have been surprised that the rest of it unfolded more or less the way it did. Denis and Paul bound Frank's and Bessie's hands with duct tape, as they had Amy's, and covered the couple's heads with pillowcases to cut down the spatter. Frank was loudly begging them not to do it, so they shot him first to shut him up, and then they shot Bessie, who had remained silent since the end of the phone call with Stevie. They stuffed the bodies of the couple and the bloodied pillowcases into a pair of black, heavy-duty, seventy-gallon garbage bags and dragged them from the windowless room out to the garage, where Paul lifted the bags one by one and gently placed them into the bed of the pickup truck. They brought out Frank's and Bessie's suitcase and two of the dead batteries from the storage room and put them in the truck beside the bags.

They tossed the mostly uneaten pizza into the dumpster behind the garage and with a mop and hose washed the remaining bits of blood and brain matter into the floor drain. A quick cursory cleanup was all. Earlier they had removed Frank's guns from the false bottom of Denis's truck bed and locked them in a metal cabinet in the garage basement with the intention of using them as collateral to pay off some of their debt to the West End Gang. A stash of American guns was worth a lot more in Canada than in America. They dropped Frank's cellphone into the drawer of the garage workbench where they had stashed Frank's and Bessie's credit cards and passports and driver's licenses. They didn't seem worried about leaving so much physical and forensic evidence at the garage. The two Canadians were sociopaths, but as Frank had observed early on, they were not very bright.

It was late, between midnight and one a.m., and most of the city of Granby was asleep, so no one saw them drive from the garage, past the deserted, darkened Autodrome and then east on Route 139 for four miles to Yamaska National Park. If anyone did take note of their departure, no one reported it then or later—a pair of local workmen in a gray Ford F-150 after a night of billiards at Dooley's, maybe, or bowling at the Salon De Quilles Quillorama, headed for home somewhere in the eastern outskirts of the city.

They took the turnoff for the Choinière Reservoir and drove beyond the marina to where the paved lane became dirt, then grass, and entered the woods. A mile farther on, the lane ended at a high, treeless bluff, a glacial moraine with a steep, cliff-like, fifty-foot drop-off to the surface of the lake. The water was dark and very deep down there, another fifty feet to the bottom. For years local teenagers, including the young Denis and Paul, had gathered late at night to leap off the cliff into the icy waters of the reservoir and for what they called "free parking," which meant underage drinking, smoking dope around a bonfire, and having sex with one another in their cars and pickup trucks. Eventually the police shut it down, and the teenagers moved on to more isolated free parking zones, and now no one came here day or night, except for the occasional visit from a tired, bored Granby cop looking for an easy roust at the end of his night shift or a spot to catch a nap unobserved.

Denis kept the engine running and the parking lights on, and he and Paul left the truck and hauled the body bags to the edge of the cliff and laid them on the ground. They lugged the two dead batteries over to the body bags and opened first one bag and then the other and shoved a battery into each and retied them. Together they grabbed the first bag at the head and the foot. They didn't know whether it contained Frank's body or Bessie's. They swung it once, twice, three times, and flung it out from the edge of the cliff into empty space and heard the splash as it hit the water far below. Then the second bag. Then the suitcase.

A half hour later they were back at the garage, and Denis suddenly remembered that they had neglected to take Frank's wallet and had forgotten to remove their prescription medicines from the suitcase. He said nothing to Paul, and told himself that the bodies and the suitcase wouldn't ever be found anyhow. And even if the murdered bodies of the couple were discovered someday by a bottom-fishing canoeist or a kid diving dangerously deep from the cliff, and the corpses and the contents of the suitcase were identified as belonging to Franklin and Elizabeth Dent of Sam Dent, New York, there would be nothing to connect their deaths to a couple of stock-car mechanics running a garage next to the Autodrome in Granby, Quebec.

Nothing, that is, except Franklin and Elizabeth Dent's grandson, Steven Dent. Arrested for the murder of his mother, young Dent made the bizarre claim that his grand-parents had been kidnapped by his mother's Canadian boy-friend. His claim was later confirmed by the fingerprints of Denis Picard, 43, and his accomplice, Paul Corbin, 41, found at the grandparents' home, and Denis Picard's fingerprints on the ATM machine at the Stewart's shop in the town of Sam Dent, and the credit and debit card PIN numbers in Franklin Dent's handwriting on the paper towel extracted from the Stewart's dumpster, and the tracking and call data on Franklin Dent's cellphone, discovered in a drawer along with the couple's passports and driver's licenses at Denis Picard's and Paul Corbin's garage in Granby, Que-bec, plus forensic evidence collected at the garage, along with the firearms stolen from the couple's Sam Dent, New York, home and transported illegally to Canada, where they were apparently sold to members of the West End Gang in Montreal and later traced back to Denis Picard and Paul Corbin and from there to the home of the elderly American couple—all of which, testimony, data, and physical evidence, was gathered and analyzed and presented by American and Canadian police investigators to a Canadian prosecutor, who used it to induce a Granby grand jury to indict Denis Picard and Paul Corbin for the kidnapping and murder of Franklin and Elizabeth Dent, even without submitting as evidence the bodies of the kidnapped and murdered victims themselves.

It wasn't until April 12, 2021, seven months after the two auto mechanics were tried and convicted and given consec-utive life sentences without parole, that the bodies of the elderly American couple were discovered. A pair of young male speed skaters who were training on the Choinière Reservoir for the 2022 Beijing Winter Olympics broke through the thinning ice a few weeks too late in the season and drowned, and the wet-suited team of Royal Canadian Navy Clearance Divers sent to bring up the skaters' bodies also found and retrieved the bodies of Franklin and Elizabeth Dent and their suitcase.

On August 17, 2019, the morning after the night that his grandparents were kidnapped and murdered in Granby, Quebec, Steven Dent, 20, confessed to the murder of his mother, Amy Dent, 39, in Plattsburgh, New York. Two Plattsburgh police officers, following up on a tip from a Plattsburgh State student they had arrested the following morning for smoking marijuana in public, had gone to apartment 3F at 422 Hamilton Street, where they found the body of Amy Dent. Her second-floor neighbor, Vincent Bradley, 56, a retired city bus driver on full disability, gave the officers a detailed description of a young man who had visited apartment 3F a few hours earlier. Bradley, who had long suspected his neighbor of selling illegal drugs out of her home, had made a practice of writing down the plate numbers of the vehicles of people visiting apartment 3F. He gave the police the number of the young man's Ford F-150 pickup truck, which turned out to be registered in the name of Franklin Dent, Steven Dent's grandfather.

At 11:45 p.m. the night of the sixteenth, two state police troopers from the Ray Brook base knocked on the door of the Irish Hill home of Franklin and Elizabeth Dent in the town of Sam Dent. When their grandson, Steven Dent, opened the door, the troopers asked to speak with

Franklin Dent, and Steven told them that his grandparents were not at home, because they had been kidnapped by a Canadian man named Denis. He readily admitted that he, not his grandfather, had driven the Ford F-150 registered to his grandfather to apartment 3F at 422 Hamilton Street earlier that evening. He went there in search of his mother, he said. But she wasn't at home, so he left. He confessed to having seen a woman's dead body at the apartment, but he didn't know whose it was. Her face was covered, he said, but he was sure that it wasn't the body of his mother, who was a much larger person. He said he hadn't called the police, because while he was at the apartment he received a phone call from his grandparents' kidnapper that had greatly upset him.

The officers drove him to the county seat in Elizabethtown, where the two of them and a detective interrogated him in a room not unlike the windowless room where his grandparents had been held in Granby. Stevie could not think of anyone he could call to advise him. His grandparents were in Canada, and the officers told him that his mother was dead. He did not know the name of a lawyer. He was alone in the interrogation room with the state troopers and the detective for six hours.

By dawn he had confessed to the murder of his mother, Amy Dent. His confession was taped and transcribed, and he signed it. In it he stated that he shot his mother because she was a drug dealer and was trying to corrupt him into becoming one himself, and in addition he was angry at her for having abandoned him when he was a child after his father was killed in Iraq. He said that the gun he used to

kill her had belonged to his grandfather, and he had tossed
it along with the drugs that his mother wanted him to sell
into the Ausable River from the bridge at Ausable Chasm.
Despite an extensive effort to locate them, the gun and
the drugs were never recovered by the police. The public defender assigned to represent young Dent at his trial
urged him to plead guilty in exchange for a twenty-year
sentence, which he did. He is currently serving his sentence at the Clinton Correctional Facility in Dannemora,
New York, where every morning he goes eagerly to his job
in the laundry room.

These days, when I walk with my dog on the winding path
that my wife and I have made and maintained up along the
wooded slope behind our house, I often think about the
Dent family, Frank and Bessie and Amy and Chip and little
Stevie. I think about the tangled branches of their family
tree all the way back to its taproot, the original Sam Dent,
for whom our town, at the founder's vainglorious insis-
tence, is named. And I think about how, with the passage of
time, a forest primeval becomes a modern woods, and how
native people are replaced by locals, how first growth gets
displaced by second and third growth, overstory by understory, how towering oak and chestnut trees are replaced
by shrubby alder, scrub pine, and poplar, and how over the
years our path through the woods undulates and meanders
in response to our tramping and rain and snowmelt, how
it absorbs alternate routes and bypasses made by the deer

and coyotes and bears, who are more sensitive to the lift and fall of the land than we are, and how the footpath itself, like the long, complicated story of a family, charts its own route uphill from the house through the thicket to the ridge and traverses the ridge to the downslope and switchbacks along a serpentine route, where the family dog has already arrived and waits by the door for us to emerge from the woods and enter the house.

A NOTE ON THE TYPE

This book is set in Iowan Old Style, a typeface designed by John Downer. It is a contemporary interpretation of Jenson, which derives from a fifteenth-century typeface designed by Nicholas Jenson. Its taller lower case letters make it suitable for both print and digital use. Iowan Old Style was released by Bitstream in 1991.

Typeset by Scribe, Philadelphia, Pennsylvania
Printed and bound by Berryville Graphics, Berryville, Virginia
Designed by Maggie Hinders